A QUESTION OF LOYALTY

A
Question
of
Loyalty

JUDITH HAWKINS

TATE PUBLISHING
AND ENTERPRISES, LLC

Published by Tate Publishing & Enterprises, LLC
127 E. Trade Center Terrace | Mustang, Oklahoma 73064 USA
1.888.361.9473 | www.tatepublishing.com

Tate Publishing is committed to excellence in the publishing industry. The company reflects the philosophy established by the founders, based on Psalm 68:11,
"The Lord gave the word and great was the company of those who published it."

Book design copyright © 2014 by Tate Publishing, LLC. All rights reserved.
Cover design by Rtor Maghuyop
Interior design by Joana Quilantang

Published in the United States of America

ISBN: 978-1-62746-320-1
1. Fiction / Christian / Romance
2. Fiction / Christian / Suspense
13.11.13

DEDICATION

To all the wonderful people who helped me craft this book: Beryl, Harold, and Jeff Hawkins; Grant Norton, US Coast Guard, and his wonderful family; "Captain" Bob Holstrand; Lynn Guise; and Kiran Spees.

As always to my Lord Jesus Christ from Whom all blessings flow.

CONTENTS

PROLOGUE

The soldiers stood side by side in the cemetery, looking down on the grave. This was not the grave of a fallen comrade. The tiny marker named its occupant as Anna Zoblecova. There was nothing else, no adornments, just a bleak cemetery on the edge of a small village in the Ukraine. The grief sculpted on the strong male faces was the only monument to this woman's life – that and the child in whose birth she had given her life.

"Sergei," the big soldier's voice cracked as speech was forced through a throat constricted with pain, "I must find the child. How could her own grandfather have given her to the State to rear? How?"

He turned to his boyhood friend, his question raised in a primal cry, taking comfort in the rock solid, silent presence of the friend who had loved this woman as much as he had, this man who had loved them both enough to give her up. This comrade had endured at his side the horrors of training in the Spetsnaz, the dreaded Soviet Special Forces. Then, together again in Afghanistan, they had won the trust of native villagers in the remote mountainous areas where Afghan guerrillas had their strongholds. Nickolai's one simple act of kindness, rescuing the child of a village leader who had fallen into a steep ravine, had won the hearts of that village. Nickolai's reputation had spread from village to village so that he and Sergei were rewarded with rare and valuable intelligence.

The very value of their unique intelligence had kept them in the field too long to help Anna! They had both hoped that they could earn their way back to her, to ensure proper medical care. It had all been too late. Nothing had ever been enough. The more they accomplished, the more was asked. They had not come to Anna in time to say goodbye or for Nicolai to give the child her rightful name. Her own family had disowned her and would not even keep the child when the authorities brought her to them as an orphan.

The child! The father's heart within him twisted in agony. He must find her, his little one, his little girl child.

"Sergei, will you help me? Will you help me find Anna's child – my child, my daughter? Sergei, say you will help me!"

Sergei's shocked numbness gave way to a blade of white-hot fury as he turned to the man who had once been dearer to him than his own brother, the man he had continued to treat as friend for Anna's sake. Now Anna was gone, killed by the lust of the pig who asked his help. Only the last months of harsh discipline in Afghanistan kept the fury from his facial expression. Death would be too kind for this defiler of women, this man who stole the woman he loved and then killed her with his seed. A quick-silver plan began to develop as the plea for help registered in Sergei's formidable intellect. Death was too good. Nicolai must suffer as Sergei now suffered.

"Yes, Comrade," he smiled slowly, as ice-cold resolve froze his heart, "I will help you find your child." He endured the pig's embrace, the embrace of a drowning man clinging to his last hope for survival.

"There is only one way, though. We can never accomplish this in the strict discipline of the Spetsnaz. The KGB has approached me. They are interested in both of us. We made a reputation in Afghanistan. Now, we must accept the recruitment of the KGB. Only by using the influence and privileges afforded to top KGB operatives will we be able to search for Anna's child. You understand? We must do as we did in Afghanistan. We must hide our true feelings and accomplish the tasks assigned to us without flinching. We must, in fact, excel. Can you do this?"

Nicolai felt his friend's words as a cold slap in the face, one he desperately needed. He pulled himself up into a pillar of iron. The friendship he had counted on for so long had proven itself once more. Sergei would help him; he must trust his friend. He could not trust anyone else. There had been times in Afghanistan when he had risked everything to protect innocents, who were just trying to raise their families but were caught in the cross-fire. He could risk such things no more.

"I will do what I have to do. I will find a way to protect and care for the daughter Anna died to give me. I will, Sergei. Believe this."

The sheer power of the man's will caused Sergei to momentarily blanch. His old friend would make a formidable enemy. But the white hot rage returned as the memory of Anna's dancing blue eyes and curling raven hair seared his heart with loss. No! Fear would not hold him back. He had survived Spetsnaz. He knew no fear. The vile pig would pay. And he, Sergei Illyvich Polyev, would doubly gain. He had been directed to reel the resourceful Nicolai Androvich Gorgonov into the KGB fold. He had reeled quite successfully, and rewards would surely follow. Then, one day, Nicolai's secret would put him in Sergei's clutches. Anna would be avenged. The vile pig would pay. Sergei knew the tool he must use to exact that payment: the child....

CHAPTER ONE

"Mother needs you." A gruff whisper from behind her right ear froze Marta Alexander in place, her sandwich halfway to her mouth.

"When Mother calls I will answer," she responded like an automaton, the result of years of KGB indoctrination.

"Be on the Bremerton ferry to Seattle tomorrow at 4:15. You will be contacted."

She heard the sound of retreating footsteps on the wooden planks of the gazebo that sheltered her picnic lunch. A car started; still her sandwich remained suspended halfway to her mouth. Slowly, her arm came down, unconsciously laying the partially eaten sandwich neatly on the picnic table in front of her. Marta Alexander had just been counting herself blessed as she looked out over Dyes Inlet. The sun was peeking out from behind the gray curtain, a rare thing in Silverdale, Washington. The green of the Evergreen State was shimmering brilliance as courageous rays danced off the mist-shrouded conifers. She'd had her favorite park to herself. All around were signs of a boom town, prosperity showing itself in a well-developed waterfront. Her photography business was booming along with the town. There had been no Soviet Union and KGB to terrorize her for so long she barely remembered their influence. She had watched walls come down, women and children stand up to tanks. She had truly believed that she was finally free to begin really living. A few seconds was all the exchange had taken, a few seconds that shattered her life.

She had always promised herself that if the KGB ever remembered her, she would go straight to the FBI. She'd thought she'd never need to do that and all the intensity of her childhood and youth were like dim dreams that had happened to someone else. Her courage was dulled with years of freedom from fear. Even seeing the looting of KGB headquarters and having various files floating around in unknown places hadn't concerned her much. The various sleeper spies uncovered on both sides had never, to her knowledge, had anything to do with her. It was all old business.

Why now? More important, who now? Who would even know about her anymore and why would they need to activate a sleeper spy? She shouldn't have hoped. She shouldn't have dreamed. It was too painful when everything shattered. It didn't matter who it was who was activating her. They knew her terrible secret and she knew they were dangerous people whoever they were. Dangerous people were probably watching her right now to see if she would follow instructions.

So far she had done everything by the book, waiting for the contact to clear the area. Marta gave herself a determined shake, reality check time. No one need know she was numb with horror.

She calmly gathered her lunch things, her camera, her photo slips showing the addresses of houses she was supposed to snap for local realtors, and her map. Then, oh so casually, she made her way to her old, battered classic VW bug. The same little car her KGB "parents" had given her when they cut her loose at 18 with instructions to wait for her "Mother" activation code.

All this flashed through her mind in seconds as she let go of it in order to move into her new reality. She had to get to the FBI offices in Seattle before 5:00 without getting killed. She couldn't afford a phone call this soon after contact. Her skills were decades rusty, but she knew she had to clear her path to make sure no one tailed her to the Bainbridge Island Ferry. It was a shorter ferry ride and her photo route took her in that direction. She checked her watch. It was just noon. She could make either the 2:05 or the 2:55 ferry and get parked before the down town Seattle traffic became totally impossible.

Perhaps, once on the ferry, she could check a phone book for the FBI contact number. She'd carried that number with her until the Soviet Union fell; she had then ceremoniously tossed it off a pier into Dyes Inlet. She sure wished she had it now. It would look much less suspicious to make a phone call with a number she already had than to look anything up in the phone book.

She finally made it to her car and started it without it blowing up. She hadn't dared check the undercarriage for a bomb. They probably wouldn't try to blow her up until after she didn't do what they wanted her to do. She followed her photo route through the many circuitous country roads between Silverdale and the main road through Poulsbo, across the Agate Passage Bridge and on to Bainbridge Island. It was a straight shot to the ferry, but if anyone could follow her as she meandered through North Kitsap County, she deserved to be shot.

As she pulled into the line waiting for the ferry, Marta was as sure as anyone could ever be that she had cleared her path. She couldn't assume she was home free. The KGB, or whoever they were, could be just paranoid enough to have stationed people on the ferries in case she decided to do exactly what she intended to do – throw herself on the mercy of the FBI. She opted out of phoning ahead to the FBI offices, having made the 2:05 ferry. She'd have plenty of time to get there before 5:00. This way, she could stay in her car to avoid as much contact as possible. With nothing to do but think, her past came back to haunt her.

She should have gone to the FBI as soon as her KGB "parents" had cut her lose with the VW, $1000.00, and the camera she'd used in her surveillance training. The skills she was relying on now for her very life would not have been so rusty then. She would have had more credibility then. With each year she had waited, her case as an unwilling KGB agent became less and less believable. They hadn't believed her when she'd tried to tell them at ten, when her "parents" first explained the harsh realities of life to her. Who could blame them? Who would believe some little kid calling to say her parents were KGB agents, raising her as a sleeper spy? The agent asked to speak to her parents. She hung up the phone without further identifying herself. Then she'd lived in terror for months, fearing that they'd been able to identify her as the caller.

Instead of calling again, she'd driven out of Tacoma and found what looked like a safe little farming town, with a small mall, and a rustic setting. She settled in, using every last dime she had including the $1000.00 she'd been given to get an apartment and set up a real estate photography business. She started taking pictures of houses, rented dark room use from a local photo shop to process them, and brought the finished product to a couple of realtors. They'd loved her technique. Word spread quickly and the rest was history. Her trusty old camera had died just in time to replace it with a digital that paid her back every time she didn't have to rent darkroom space.

Marta saw the Seattle ferry dock looming up before her and nearly panicked as the ferry closed in on the terminal. She wondered whether it was better to be shot by the FBI or the KGB clones. She sincerely hoped the FBI didn't resort to torture. She had no doubt about the KGB. The FBI was definitely the better risk. She followed the car in front of her off the ferry and went to look for a parking space so she could clear her path to the Federal Building, just two blocks up from the ferry terminal.

She parked at the far end of the glitzy Seattle waterfront, very close to the Seattle Center where the famous Space Needle resides. It was no small task to walk back to the Federal Building, but her well-honed runner's body made good time in spite of the circuitous route, up-hill and down, through the downtown library and back to Second Avenue. She stopped one last time at a crosswalk across from her goal, subtly checking around her for anyone watching too closely or being a bit too alert.

Matt Barton rubbed the back of his neck, sore from endless hours of pouring over the same Homeland Security intelligence information. As compelling as the case was, it couldn't hold his attention. He kept remembering that woman in the cafeteria this morning. He'd noticed her when she walked in. Every guy there had noticed her, but she had focused right in on him. Why? Why did it always have to be him? He, along with every other red blooded male in the place, had watched her as she made her sensuous way across the room toward his table. Her eyes had locked on his. He hadn't been able to look away. His mouth had gone dry. His body had gone on auto-pilot. Swallowing became a major enterprise.

Her perfume arrived subtly before her physical presence and collided with his senses. She put her tray down and smiled the smile of a conqueror. He just tried to keep breathing, but not too hard. He wanted to jump up and run, but instead he started praying. She started speaking. Just friendly chit-chat, confident she had him. No one in that entire room had any doubt that he was her target and she had hit a bull's eye. Somehow he answered the small talk out loud as he prayed internally for the strength to get up and walk away without getting this woman's phone number or, worse, just walking out of there with her. Somehow he managed to finish his coffee almost as if he were a sane man. He had laid his napkin on his tray with painstaking care. He had smiled at her and wished her a good day. The absolutely incredulous look on her face made him pause. This was going to hurt her, humiliate her. It was obvious that she had never had a man walk away like this before. He picked up his tray knowing he had to get away, sending a plea to the Lord to save her some embarrassment as he walked away. Then inspiration hit. He turned back, just for a second.

"You know," he had said with just the right amount of awe in his voice, not worship, not surrender, just awe, "you are one of the most beautiful women I have ever seen in my life. You really made my day when you sat down across from an ordinary guy like me." He'd sent her a brilliant smile and managed to leave the cafeteria without falling over anything. It had cost him. It cost him every time it happened, and it happened way too often. It was taking its toll.

"Twenty years, Lord," Matt groaned in silent prayer. "Twenty years since I made the covenant with my youth group pastor and youth group to maintain sexual purity until marriage. Every one of the rest of that group is married, some with children as old as I was when I made the covenant. This morning is just one time. You know that Lord. I'm actually getting a reputation as a playboy because of the pointed attentions of attractive women. Honest, I can't take much more. Gwen is a sweet woman, Lord, who loves you. Why can't she be the one that you give me for a wife? Why do you continue to confirm to us that we are to wait for another when we're such good friends? I know we haven't known each other that long, and she's older than I, and she didn't keep herself for marriage, but she repented and returned to You. You've forgiven and cleansed. You can overcome any obstacles. I'm willing. She's willing. What gives, Lord?"

Matt took a deep cleansing breath, "Sorry, Lord. I'm trying to take control again. I gave myself to you and accept Your will. I don't regret that decision for a second. I trust You. I will wait on You and renew my strength by Your grace, but I really don't think I'm going to get much work done today."

Matt sighed and got back to the information before him. A part of his new duties as the Assistant Special Agent-in-Charge was to screen such cases for assignment to a section. Before 9/11 this would have been easy, Foreign Counter Intelligence Section. Post 9/11, however, the lines were blurred and the tendency was to assume terrorism first and foreign intelligence second. He could see why both the military and Homeland Security, even the CIA who usually shared nothing, were worried about a pattern of information leaks that seemed to center in taverns around military installations as places of recruitment and information gathering. The kicker was that it matched a pattern that emerged about 20 years ago in KGB recruitment and espionage. What had started as GRU and KGB activity in village tea houses in Afghanistan had then spread to taverns around American military bases around the world.

KGB agents actually purchased businesses and information seemed to flow easily from the unwary customers. The best businesses were those that invited patrons to come in and stay awhile for relaxing conversation and whatever stimulant that would keep that conversation bubbling up in good fellowship. Thus taverns and tea houses seemed to have been the major targets. That activity appeared to have stopped after the fall of the Soviet Union, the dissolution of the KGB and the chaos that ensued. Now the pattern had reemerged in Afghanistan and Iraq. No big surprise, one could assume there were still some folks with either Soviet training or keen observation who picked up the technique. But it began to emerge again around American bases, as well as their ally's bases, around the world. And here in the Seattle area, where so many sensitive military installations were clustered.

Had the technique leaked into terrorist training camps second hand? Or was the mastermind behind the technique actively training terrorists? Or was it terrorists at all? Or had China or North Korea picked up on it? There was a lot of money to be made in information and the Russian mafia was not averse to making it any way it could be made. A lot of former KGB had disappeared into the criminal underworld or were selling their expertise and any arms they could get hold of to the highest bidder. That brought in elements of organized crime and even drug cartels. After all, the war in Afghanistan affected more than just the oil trade. Matt's head spun with the options, each complicating the assignment of the case more than the last.

Matt's aching neck finally drove him to stand up and go to the window for another people-watching break. One of the perks of his new promotion was his very own private office with walls and a door and even a window! You couldn't see much detail from this height, but you could get a feel for what was happening down there. Traffic was gearing up for the late afternoon rush hour. The bus stops were starting to pile up with people. He glanced across the street and froze. The hair on the back of his neck stood out, and he couldn't for the life of him understand why. By instinct, premonition, or divine inspiration, an internal nudge he'd learned not to ignore, he knew something was going on down there. He got out his binoculars.

He saw her then, a tall brunette, well-built, with runner's legs. She was waiting to cross the street from the north. She was too alert, and she was checking out the scene around her. For just a second he caught her full face, a perfect oval with winged black brows over vivid azure eyes. Her hair framed her face in dark wisps; it was piled precariously in a topknot. She was stunning, a classic beauty.

"Oh no, Lord, just what I need. She's more beautiful than the one this morning. I'm losing it."

Yet, he followed her with the binoculars until she joined the crowd crossing the street. He swept the area around her for signs of someone tailing her. It seemed vital to him that he do so. He hoped no one would come in and see him doing this. He wouldn't be able to explain. He couldn't even explain it to himself. He only knew it was vital. He couldn't spot anything, but something nagged at him. Something was wrong. He thought about getting the camera with the telephoto on it and snapping some shots of the street below, but that was way over the top. Besides, whatever had been there would be gone by the time he got a camera. He laid the field glasses aside but continued to stare out the window.

Those azure eyes kept haunting him. He'd never seen such blue, blue eyes. They were enough to haunt any man, but that wasn't what haunted him now. She was in danger. He could sense it, and, beyond all reason, he ached to help her.

"Why so glum, Matt?" Jumping at the sound, Matt turned to Frank Monroe, as the Special Agent-in-Charge laughed. "Don't you like rain? It rained in the Florida Keys didn't it?"

"Oh, yeah, it rained there all right, but it was warm, and you didn't mind so much. Then again, the sun did occasionally break through. I tell you, Frank, I'm losing my tan. This is getting serious."

"Don't worry about the tan. Rust is about the same color, and you're flinty enough to rust quite nicely here."

"Frank," Matt broke in with precision, "flint doesn't rust."

"Okay, okay. So, what besides losing your tan is getting to you?" Frank grinned mischievously, "I hear you were vamped by one of Seattle's super models this morning in the cafeteria. She seemed to think your tan was just fine. The way I hear it, she might have wanted to compare tan lines."

Matt groaned, shaking his head, "A super model? You've got to be kidding. This is doing nothing to dispel my reputation as a playboy, and nobody ever earned it less."

"If only they knew that they accuse the most virginal man I know," Frank eyes twinkled, showing that he thought more of Matt for his strong stand for purity. Frank had introduced him to his wonderful church when Matt had moved up from Florida, and now they both worked with the youth. Matt shared pretty openly about his own covenant as he encouraged the young people to believe that true love was worth the wait.

"And, yes," Frank continued, "she was a super model. She graced our lowly domain in order to renew her passport. So aside from surviving temptations that would make most men grovel and plead for mercy, what's bothering you? You're frowning out that window like the fate of the free world is hanging on your next move."

Matt felt a sudden chill at those words. He gave a weak chuckle, shaking his head, "I guess I'm not the only guy in the free world who has a nervous stomach over this 'super-case' that the military, the CIA, and even Homeland Security have deviated from their usual habits and are eager to share with us."

"Having trouble with the transition to assigning cases rather than working in the field?" Frank's eyes twinkled outrageously. Frank and Matt went back a long way. Matt had been privy to some of Frank's disquiet as he made the transition from the field.

"Guilty," Matt chuckled. "It's tough to leave an open-ended case like this. I feel like we're so close, like the very next corner I turn will give us the right info to set up a sting. The military wants it and Homeland Security wants it. CIA doesn't have jurisdiction, so they want us to set up a sting. And, yes, I want it. I'd love to take point on a case like this," Matt said, hanging his head.

"It's a major transition, and it takes time. You can't work on every case. You have to set priorities on which cases really need your personal attention and which can be delegated to team leader in one of the sections. That's not all of it, though, is it? That little altercation this morning with the super model make you wish you'd have accepted the invitation? Maybe it's time you and Gwen moved past friendship. It's better to marry than to burn, don't you know?" Frank winked.

Matt ground his teeth and silently asked the Lord if He'd heard that. "I didn't know she was a super model, and Gwen and I are fine. If you really want to know what's bothering me, answer me this. If you were trying to assign this case where would you put it: Foreign Counterintelligence, Terrorism, Organized Crime? That's what I've been going over. We don't have it defined enough yet to assign to a section. I really need a cross-functional team with experts in multiple areas and that's a team I'd really like to lead myself."

"Good analysis, ASAC Barton. Set up your team and take point," Frank's grin spread as Matt's jaw dropped. "I was actually coming in to discuss that scenario with you. I'm glad you reached the same conclusion on your own. Since you're a brother, would you like to pray over it with me? Then we can trust the Lord for the rest."

"I'd love to," Matt was sure his relief was obvious to his friend, brother, and boss, as they bowed their heads for a quick prayer for guidance.

As Matt lifted his head from prayer and he opened his eyes to the street scene he and his boss were both looking at during the prior discussion. His whole body tensed as he looked intensely at the intersection across the street.

"Hey, what's the matter?" Frank asked.

"I don't know. It's a pattern, the way a couple of people were standing." Matt shook his head and came down a little from red alert. He no longer saw the girl, but something wasn't right. "I guess I'm just full of gut feelings today. I'd have sworn there were a couple of pro's out there."

"Maybe they're some reassigned agents. We can always use more. Better yet, it may be a bevy of super models heading up here to test your mettle," Frank laughed, as if trying to break the tension in the younger man. "Let it go, Matt. I can't afford to send you on rest leave."

Matt really laughed this time. Rest leave was an old joke between them. They'd been on a case with an agent they'd admired less than a little. After weeks of grueling leg work, this bozo had requested a rest leave right at the crucial moment, as if everyone else wasn't burnt to a crisp. That agent didn't last long in the FBI. "Can you spare me time for a cup of coffee and a sandwich? It's four already, and I haven't worked up the nerve to go back to the cafeteria all day."

"Okay, you can go to the cafeteria. Flirt with all the super models you want, and even go to the little boy's room, but then you must promise to come back and get some real work done."

"Yes, Sir." Matt gave a comic salute and started out of the office with Frank.

Nicolai Androvich Gorgonov watched as little Marta entered the Federal Building. "Little Marta?" he chuckled to himself. She was all grown up now, and precious little he'd had to do with it. Too little…too late. No time for regrets. She had done well clearing her path, but not well enough, for here he was. If he could follow, perhaps others, far more dangerous than he, could follow as well. But then, she was doing exactly as he had expected and hoped that she would do. After all, she had not been raised in the Ukraine. She knew only the KGB. She had no memories to haunt her of the deep, rich soil of home, the longing to smell again the wind off the Dnieper River, to hear its music. Nicolai knew this longing, but he had been a child there. He had dug his hands deep in the soil and longed to farm, as his ancestors had farmed before him, on the same plot of land.

No, Marta had been a child here. Her roots were here in American and so, evidently, was her loyalty. He had intended this, his own little counter-sleeper spy that he'd hoped never to activate. He could manage her flight to the FBI, for he had something the FBI wanted very badly: Himself and all he knew. If it came down to it, he would barter himself for her freedom. After all, who was he betraying now? "Mother Russia?" He laughed to himself. He was Ukrainian. He had his own country now. He still wasn't quite sure who was in charge there, but then he didn't quite know who was in charge in Russia either. More importantly, who controlled the information and the assets of the former KGB? Putin was the figure head in Russia, but what power was really behind him?? Always the puppet, never the puppet master, that man. What hope there was for his poor homeland, he did not know. What hope there was for him anywhere, he did not know. He had managed to stay under everyone's radar for over a decade and move like a shadow among men, as his code name indicated was his greatest talent. But even the great Shadow himself could not remain invisible forever. There is always something that will draw even the most careful of men from their hiding place.

Oh, he had cheered at the fall of the Communist powers in his homeland and hoped that his own shadow organization had chipped away at its foundations enough to have contributed to that fall. He had also watched as information from the KGB headquarters had fled in the hands of many desperate people, some he recognize, amazed they would risk their faces on international television, and some he did not. One he knew and whose face had wisely been hidden from all cameras had brought to him his file along with Marta's and others. He had watched from the shadows, hoping to protect Marta from any taint. His watching was not limited to his daughter and her protection, though. From his vantage point of secrecy and skill and experience, he had seen growing a cancer on the landscape, an unholy marriage between renegade ex-KGB operatives with crime bosses and terrorists. He had been able to provide quiet, secret tips and hints to mitigate some damage, to head some assets in the right direction. Sometimes, he had been too late....he shook away the horror of airplanes diving into the Twin Towers and the Pentagon. Still, in the aftermath, he had been able to reach out from the shadows again with tips and hints, knowing those caves in Afghanistan as well as he did. Yet, he now had to focus on the immediate threat. This he could still prevent, even though it meant putting his own daughter at risk to do so.

Marta Alexander stood nervously at the intersection, willing the light to change quickly. This was the critical moment if anyone was watching her. Once she was inside the Federal Building across the street, it would be too late for anyone to make a move to stop her. It was like a slice out of a nightmare, stretching out infinitely long, though only a few seconds, but her plan was firm. If she made it into the building alive, she would tell the FBI the whole thing and ask them what she should do. As if in answer to her resolve, the light changed. She made her way across to the Federal Building and got through the metal detector after placing her digital camera in the basket as she passed through, mentally kicking herself for not leaving it with the car.

She felt relief, knowing that if anyone was tailing her they were probably armed and would never risk the metal detector. She found the office of the FBI listed on the marquee and located the right bank of elevators. So far, so good. The elevator signaled her floor and she plunged into the hallway, trying not to lose her nerve. She collided with a solid wall of muscle. It was, in fact, the broad chest of a rather large man. Panic set in.

CHAPTER TWO

Matt looked down into wide azure eyes as he tried to steady the young woman who had just careened into him. He wasn't prepared for the terror he found there. He immediately recognized the woman he'd seen earlier and knew that his gut instinct had been correct. She was in danger. All of his protective instincts kicked into high gear.

"Steady, now, steady," he soothed as he physically kept her from falling. "Now, how can we help you? Who are you looking for? Are you here for an appointment with someone?"

The questions only seemed to disturb her more.

"Appointment? Oh no! I should have called to make one. No, I…I must speak to someone now. Please. I've just been contacted by the KGB and I don't know what to do."

Matt nodded almost imperceptibly to the surveillance cameras guarding the entrance to the FBI's office to signal them that he was bringing someone in. Whether this was a nut case or a real live cold-war left-over nightmare, he wanted the boss to monitor it from the get-go.

"Okay, I'll listen. Let's get out of the public eye a little, though."

The receptionist must have caught his signal because she buzzed him in. He led the visibly shaking young woman into an interrogation room and pulled a comfortable chair up to the table for her. He definitely wanted to play "good cop" on this one.

"It's all right now, we'll just talk."

She looked at him as if he were her last hope in the world, and Matt felt distinctly queasy under her gaze. He noticed the camera. Ah! That must be it. She'd witnessed something and gotten it on camera. Perhaps this would be easier than he thought, in spite of his screaming instincts warning otherwise. He had a sudden flashback to the street scene that had raised his hackles just a few minutes before. Perhaps this was a set up? There's no such thing as easy, Matt warned himself.

"Do you have some photos for us?" Matt asked hopefully.

She stared down at the camera in confusion. "These are my real estate pictures."

"What!?"

"Pictures of houses. I take pictures of houses for realtors and digital multiple listing services. Oh, no," the light obviously clicked on for her, if not for Matt. "The camera has nothing to do with this. You can have it if you'd like. It's just houses," she started to hand it to him almost apologetically.

"Would you open it and take the memory card out please? Then hand it to me." Matt prayed silently, *"Oh, Lord, please don't let it be a bomb."* He couldn't believe he'd let her in here with this thing. He had visions of the whole floor blowing out onto Second Avenue. She popped out the memory card and handed it to him. To Matt's great relief there was no explosion.

That little activity seemed to calm her immensely. She settled back and looked ready to speak rationally as she watched him take the camera and the card to the door and pass it out to Frank's waiting hands. Frank turned and handed them to one of Matt's favorite co-workers, a little wren of a woman.

"Jane, would you process this stuff for us, carefully if you would please?" Frank instructed. "I'm going to get Matt and his guest a cup of coffee and join them."

Matt turned back to the young woman, "Would you like some coffee?"

"Decaf, please." Frank heard and went to get what would hopefully be a soothing drink for all concerned. Matt could sure use some soothing.

"My name's Matt," he reached out to shake hands. She stood and shook his hand firmly.

"I'm Marta Alexander," she responded as Frank returned expertly balancing three cups of coffee and set them on the conference table without spilling a drop. Matt envied him his calm composure.

"I'm Frank, Marta. And the cup nearest you is the decaf. Matt and I tend to remain caffeinated will into the afternoon," he grinned.

They all took seats around the table, Frank leaning back with his hands behind his head in the most relaxed posture Matt had ever seen. He found himself calming just watching Frank stretch out and found his own posture relaxing. Basic interviewing technique and Matt was embarrassed to have to be reminded of it. He purposefully relaxed his posture and turned to Marta.

"Okay, Marta, tell me what's on your mind," Matt encouraged.

Marta focused on the FBI agent across from her to monitor his body language as she tried to tell her story and remain credible at the same time. She decided to tell it exactly as it occurred this afternoon and fill in the background as she went.

"I was contacted by the KGB this morning with my recognition code and told to take the 4:00 p.m.ferry from Bremerton to Seattle tomorrow for further instructions. I haven't seen or heard from anyone in the KGB since they 'graduated' me at eighteen. I've never been in an operation; I was trained and told to wait until I was contacted. I had been hoping, with all the changes, they'd forgotten about me." Her voice broke as she paused to gain control again. She was unable to determine anyone's body language with tears swimming in her eyes so she focused on getting rid of those.

"How did you get involved with the KGB in the first place?" The agent who called himself Frank asked in the kindest voice Marta had ever heard. She wondered if it was sincere or a very good interrogation technique.

"I'm not really sure. I was raised by two people who told me that I'd been smuggled into the United States by the KGB. At first, I thought they had just flipped out. I mean, it was nuts. We didn't have much of a family life, but I knew other kids who didn't either. I didn't really think about it. I was a kid; they were my parents. Then, other people got involved, and they started training me, indoctrinating me."

"Who were some of these other people? Can you remember any names?" the agent who called himself Matt asked, in a similarly kind and conversational tone. Yes, she remembered practicing such a tone in her training.

"Oh, other tavern owners sometimes came over or we went over there or went on a camping trip as a group. The guy I called Dad owned a tavern across from Joint Base Lewis McChord. My folks spent a lot of time there. My favorite trainer was Uncle Nicky. Sometimes he and I would sneak off and have a play day. He said that was important, too. He'd take me to the zoo or for ice cream. Of course, he taught me stuff on the way, like how to spot and lose a tail."

Both agents nodded, acknowledging her little chuckle, as if hers was the most normal story they'd ever heard.

"The lady I called Mom was the real trainer. She taught me the martial arts, weapons use, surveillance techniques, how to identify a 'hook' to get someone obligated or scared enough to give you information or do what you wanted. The others didn't have much to do with me. They just faded in and out. I only remember one other kid and she was a whole lot younger than I."

"Did anyone seem to be in charge?" Matt asked.

Marta thought a moment, "I'm not sure, but I'd say Uncle Nicky was the real heavyweight, even though he was the nicest to me. He had an aura of authority. I know Peter, my 'dad,'" Marta slurred *dad* out sarcastically, "seemed to bristle when he came around, but he never challenged him. Tanya, my mom," no sarcasm this time, "kind of used Uncle Nicky as a control on

Peter. She gave me an emergency phone number once. One of the emergencies she defined for me was Peter getting out of line. I called the number once, just to see what would happen. Uncle Nicky answered on the first ring and, once he found out I was all right, he told me to be sure I only called in a real emergency. I've never called it again."

"Do you still have it?" Frank's voice finally showed some intensity.

Marta hesitated. This was more than she'd bargained for. Doing in the KGB was one thing, but Uncle Nicky was quite another.

"He's the only one who was ever really nice to me. I know it's crazy, but I don't want him hurt."

"The Soviet Union fell and the KGB was disbanded. Do you think the number is still operable?" Matt asked calmly…neither agent showed any more intensity, must have gotten it back under control, but something about the number was sure interesting to them.

"I can't explain it, but yes. I think Uncle Nicky has kept that number just in case I need to call him. Don't ask me why. I felt he protected me back then, and I kind of like to think he still is. I'd hate to hurt him now."

"You've never called the number since that one time?" Frank reiterated.

"No," Marta shook her head. "I've been tempted a few times, especially those first years when things were really rough. Money was short. I was worried that Peter or someone equally nasty would contact me at any moment. And sometimes I just got really lonely."

"We'll get back to the number later," Matt intervened as Marta started to tear up again. "Go on with what led up to today's incident."

"Basically, Peter and Tanya cut me loose at eighteen and told me to wait for my recognition code."

"And what was the code?" Frank asked.

"*Mother needs you.* My response is: *When Mother calls, I will answer.*"

"Did you give that answer today?" Matt's question this time, evidently they were taking turns. She wondered if "good cop, bad cop" would come into play any time soon, and then had to keep back a giggle. She thought she might be getting hysterical.

"Yes, I never thought about it. It just came out. He came up behind me, and I responded like one of Pavlov's dogs. I never even tried to see him. I just wanted him to go away."

Marta studied Matt, the agent across from her to try and regain some control as panic tried to take her again. She knew he was large because she was no half-pint at 5'8", and she had to look up to find his face when they collided in the lobby. Once she'd found it, his deep brown eyes captured her in their golden sparkles. For the barest second, she thought she saw surprised recognition. That fleeting expression melted so quickly into a warm, golden curiosity that she forgot it instantly. She felt like an idiot, yet she couldn't seem to speak. She had expected the cold, hard eyes of someone like her KGB "father" or some impersonal bureaucrat. She had not expected to run smack into the kind of warmth that drew her into a protective glow. She took in his wide forehead, topped by close-cropped, curly, brown hair; thick bushy brows over those hypnotic eyes; a straight Roman nose; and thick, sensual lips.

Marta shook herself to break the trance. Even now she could be watched. Even now she could be endangering her life and the life of these men.

"I know I should have come sooner," she stammered, catching a breath to hold back the panic. "They never told me my real name, but they did show me a picture of my family in Russia. They said terrible things would happen to those people if I didn't do exactly as I was told. It was only a picture. I know that now, but somewhere there are real people who will suffer because of me, because of my actions.

I should have come sooner. I did try to call once when I was a child, but the lady just asked to speak to my parents and I hung up. I thought about what could happen if that lady traced the call and I never had the nerve to try again. Why risk it until I was actually asked to do something that could harm America? I know it looks bad, but I just couldn't bring myself to come sooner." Marta knew she was rambling now, but couldn't seem to stop herself.

Matt, with his golden brown eyes, moved forward, almost as if to comfort her, "Okay, take a minute to pull yourself together."

The kindness was back in those big brown eyes as he spoke to her. Hope flared like fireworks on the Fourth of July. Then she felt the wet tears rolling down her cheeks, and humiliation set in. She felt the heat in her cheeks. An old lesson came back to haunt her: "Don't waste emotions. Conjure them up when they'll do the most good. American men are weak, sentimental fools. They'll do anything for a girl in tears."

"Stop!" she'd said it aloud to shut out the ugly thoughts and saw the two agents jump at her outburst. They'd think she was ready for the funny farm. A new dread clutched her. Insane asylums were where the KGB hid their recalcitrant citizens. Did the FBI do that? Both men were watching her, studying the emotions clearly displayed on her face. Another lesson came to taunt her weakness: "Wear you mask. Show no emotion. Discipline, girl, discipline!" A sharp smack had reminded her to keep her mask on, at least in front of those liars who had defiled the name of Father and Mother.

"Will you be all right alone for a moment?" Matt asked as he handed her his handkerchief. She nodded assent as she accepted yet another kindness when she should be bolstering her armor. He and the other man, Frank, stepped out of the office together. They would engage the great resources of the FBI to check on her story. A bone weary numbness spread over Marta as she sat, unmoving, wondering what new life her actions had put into motion. One thing she knew for certain, her life as she had known it had ended the moment she had crashed into the rock hard chest of a handsome FBI agent named Matt.

CHAPTER THREE

Matt and Frank stepped into the observation room on the other side of the two-way mirror in the interrogation room they'd just left. Frank studied the motionless figure in the next room.

"I don't think she's even blinked since we left. Your handkerchief is still in her hand."

Matt nodded and stepped up to the observation window. She looked so fragile, despite her strong, athlete's body.

"She's drop-dead gorgeous," Frank observed calmly. Matt envied him his calm. "I suppose a swinging bachelor like you has already noticed, though?" Frank cocked an eyebrow.

"Yes, I noticed," he said wryly, "I'm celibate, not dead." His expression turned serious as he continued, "I can't read her, Frank. She's got raw emotion on her face one minute, a mask the next. You think she's the real thing or some kook?"

"I'd bet she's no kook. Let's get her permission to tape her statement."

"Frank, remember a few minutes ago in my office? I saw her across the street, and the hair on the back of my neck stood up. I almost took pictures, but thought I was going nuts. Boy, do I wish I'd taken those pictures. Two pro's and one of them was that woman sitting in there. I'm sure of it now."

"Two pro's!? What makes you think that? Who was the other pro?"

"I'd swear there was a man tailing her. Tall, full head of grey hair, alert, but blending in…deliberately blending in, you know. He was just too intent on her. If I hadn't had the viewpoint from above, I'd never have connected the two. It was like a pattern, but I dismissed it as my imagination."

"Let's not dismiss anything now. See if you can sketch what you saw."

"I didn't catch his face. He didn't look up, she did. I couldn't see any details."

"Still, sketch out what caught your attention as well as you can. We'll try to work with that. And don't let this gal throw you. You need to get a grip, buddy."

Matt nodded curtly, knowing Frank was right. He was handling this poorly, just because of a pair of blue eyes and the nicest legs he'd ever seen. He further acknowledged an instinctive response to something he couldn't explain. His control was slipping. Two more agents stepped into the observation room, Jane Wilson and Rusty McDonough.

Jane's "drabness" fell away as her brown eyes sparkled with mischief. "Hear you bagged a real live spook, Matt! That ought to fuel your mystique around here."

Matt groaned, knowing that Jane referred to his undeserved playboy image. "Don't rub it in," Matt groused.

"Hey, rub some of it on me, won't you?" the red-headed, freckled, and wiry Rusty piped up. "Some of us could make good use of that mystique." They all chuckled knowing that Rusty would make about as much use of it as Matt did.

"Lay off," Matt elbowed his fellow agent, "I've got enough to worry about without worrying about your dismal love life." At that they all turned their attention to what he had to worry about.

Marta's numbness began to wear off as she sat in the silence. She knew deep within her that she'd done the right thing. Then she glanced to her right, noticing for the first time a mirror on the wall. All the old messages came back. Under interrogation there would always be unseen observers, perhaps cameras recording every movement, every nuance of expression to catch unguarded revelations of body language. She had come to the "good guys," and they did not own her a friend and ally. It had been a childish hope, but its lack of realism did not diminish the pain of its death.

Matt of the golden eyes returned. Marta was ready by then to go on with it, whatever it finally meant to her. There was compassion in those brown eyes, but they were guarded as well. He handed her back her camera.

"We reviewed your pictures. Lots of houses for sale over in Kitsap County," he grinned.

"I take pictures for realtors and multiple listing services. Oh, I probably told you that already. Anyway, that's why I have the camera," she finished lamely. Matt just nodded as she took back her camera.

"I'd like to continue our conversation, but would you mind if I tape it. It's much easier to remember what we've already talked about when we can review it on tape." Matt showed her a small digital recorder. She nodded her consent. "Could you give your consent verbally so we have that on tape as well?"

"Yes, of course. You have my consent to tape our conversation."

"Please give your name and a brief synopsis of why you came to us. Then proceed to tell me about your parents."

Marta took a deep breath and began anew, "My name, at least the name on my birth certificate, is Marta Alexander. I came here today because I was given my KGB activation code this morning. This code was given to me by the people who were listed as my parents on my birth certificate, Tanya and Peter Alexander. They told me that they were not my parents but were KGB sleeper spies who were raising me in the US as a sleeper spy. All the time I was with them, they were tavern owners in Tacoma. I think their business license was under Tanya and Peter Alexander. Whether those are their real names or not, I couldn't tell you. They had several sets of identity papers for the three of us. I only received one set, listing me as Marta Alexander, when they released me to go my own way at age 18.

Of the two of them, Tanya seemed the most professional, and she did most of my training. Peter would disappear from time to time, but not Tanya. She never left me alone with Peter. If they both went somewhere, Uncle Nicky stayed with me. Those were the good times. We broke every house rule we could think of. As far as information about what they were doing or why, I was never told. They were very careful about that. Uncle Nicky may have been fun, but he never slipped. He also seemed to tie things together, you know. No matter who was at the house, they all showed him respect. I think he may have been the one everyone reported to."

She watched the agent try to hide his sudden interest. She felt a real pang. Uncle Nicky had been the only bright spot in her bleak childhood. Now she was betraying him along with the others.

"Uncle Nicky started coming around after they, my 'parents,' began training me when I was ten years old. He did almost all of my training on 'clearing your path.' You understand the term?"

The agent nodded that he did.

"I think what was really happening was we were sneaking away to play. Tanya wasn't bad, you understand, but she was always so serious. She didn't play with me like Uncle Nicky did. Nobody but him seemed to have a sense of humor, or to understand mine. My sense of humor got me into trouble on more than one occasion, but never with Uncle Nicky.

Tanya introduced me to running and photography, which have been my two passions. I realize now that they both had a purpose for the KGB, but they also have meant survival to me. When I was 18, Tanya gave me $1000, my camera, and an old VW bug. That gave me a start to take care of myself.

As far as my parents' activities were concerned, they spent most of their time with people who came into the tavern. They sponsored a baseball team, complete with jackets. They had picnics for them, made up special drinks, and had reduced prices for the military and civil service folks. I think Tanya would make most of the initial contacts, and then Peter would move in. He'd get things on people and use that to control them.

They honored all credit cards at the tavern, so they had an excuse to do credit checks. I didn't get much detail, but Peter used to gloat over how stupid and gullible Americans are. Uncle Nicky was always getting mad at him if he said stuff like that in front of me. Tanya just endured him. I think she was kind of scared of him, though.

She stood up to Peter only once. He tried to take over my training. Said there were some things a woman just couldn't teach. I didn't understand what he wanted to teach me, but I'd never been so scared of anything before in my life. Tanya just stood in front of him. I think she would have killed him, or died trying. She threatened to call Nicolai, that's what they called Uncle Nicky. Peter sneered at her to go ahead and call the 'old goat.'

Uncle Nicky was there in half an hour. He told Peter that he would take care of any training that Tanya couldn't handle. Peter backed down, but he didn't like it. I heard him mutter that Uncle Nicky was an old pig, but he'd never say something like that to his face. He was scared of Uncle Nicky.

Anyway, I got a weekend trip to Lake Chelan out of it!" Marta's eyes sparkled at the memory of a whole weekend away from her oppressive home life in Uncle Nicky's company. "We just hiked and took pictures. He talked about the Ukraine. He's not Russian, you know," Marta nodded toward the agent to be sure he understood the importance of that fact in the post-Soviet world. "He mostly talked about how the soil smelled, how it felt in your hand, and what a rich harvest of crops could grow there if you treated the land right and worked with your heart. He was excited about all the irrigation going on in Eastern Washington. I think Uncle Nicky was really a farmer at heart." Matt grinned in response to her enthusiasm.

"When I got back from the weekend, Tanya asked me if there was anything I wanted to talk about. It was the kindest tone she'd ever used with me. I asked her whether the soil in the Ukraine was really that much better than the soil here. She looked relieved and showed the only glimmer of a sense of humor I'd ever seen. She said it always amazed her that a soft-hearted farmer like Nicolai could make such a good spy. She said she didn't know anything about dirt in the Ukraine and dropped the subject. She never stood up to Peter again, and he left me scrupulously alone.

I got the impression from Peter that I was a really lousy spy. That suited me fine. He said I spoke Russian like an American pig trying to grunt the mother tongue. I bungle most stuff on purpose, hoping they'd give up on me and leave me alone. Tanya may have seen through me, but Peter just thought I was dumb. He was into guns and coercion – direct confrontation. Tanya was the subtle one. As I said, she'd make the initial contacts. I thought she only brought Peter in when she needed a bully."

Marta was running out of ideas for things to say. She looked at the agent, and he helped her out.

"You said they cut you loose at eighteen," Matt commented, looked at his own hand-written notes. "Fill me in on what's been happening since then."

"I just drove out of Tacoma looking for a place to hide. I was about out of gas, when I drove into a little town called Silverdale. It looked perfect. I stopped at a Realtor's office, just on a wild chance that I could pick up a little money taking pictures of houses. As it happened, he was part of a group of realtors who'd just started an independent multiple listing. They needed a photographer. It couldn't have been more perfect. Silverdale looked like a sleepy little farming town, centrally located on the Kitsap Peninsula, so I had easy access to all other residential communities. Living was fairly cheap back then.

I didn't even realize there was a major submarine base there until I had to drive around it to get to houses for sale in that area.

It took even longer to realize that there was a Navy weapons station close by and a major Navy shipyard in downtown Bremerton. By the time I realized I was in a prime location for espionage, my business was well enough established to tie me down, but not successful enough to transplant. I was stuck. So I just hunkered down and hoped the KGB would forget about me or write me off as a bungler. When the Soviet Union fell, I figured I was home free. I guess not, huh." Marta shook her head glumly.

"Today was a test, perhaps, to see what you'd do?" Matt suggested. Marta knew then that she'd probably been followed.

"Probably," she nodded slowly; as she saw her chances of survival go from dismal to improbable.

"I must step out a moment," Matt's voice brought her back from her nightmare.

Suddenly she remembered that she still had customers waiting for their pictures to post on the MLS. "Do you know when we'll be finished here? My customers are waiting to post their new listings on the MLS until I get the pictures to them."

"I'm sorry," he shook his head, looking bewildered. "At this point, I doubt we'll be finished any time soon."

Marta realized then how idiotic she must have sounded, but she'd never let her customers down. She was holding on frantically to some sense of normality and the hope she'd be able to return to the business she'd built from her own initiative and enterprise.

"I'm sure you think I'm silly, but people are depending on me. While the KGB thing has been a dim memory, I've been focused on taking care of my customers. Please excuse me; the transition is not going smoothly."

Matt smiled as he answered, "I can understand that. The problem is I don't know when or if we'll be able to restore you to the life you've built. We'll do our best. That's all I can offer for now," he finished kindly. His kind tone warmed her heart enough that she thought she could endure this limbo, at least a little while longer.

Matt practically ran into Frank as he left the interrogation room. "Come into my office, Matt," Frank drew him along in that direction. "We've found out that the Alexanders did own a tavern across from McChord. They sold out to a corporation and disappeared after the Soviet Union fell. The corporate ownership will take some time to sort out. It's a labyrinth of corporations within corporations. I've called in the troops and we're checking out everything, especially this Uncle Nicky. If he's who I think he is, we've hit pay dirt big time. You're little problem of this afternoon may have just resolved itself most unexpectedly."

"Nicolai Androvich Gorgonov," Matt emphasized each name almost like a mantra. "The old master himself could very well be the mastermind behind the resurgence of this tavern thing. No one has ever been able to tail him, did you know that? Not even his own people, from what I hear. A defector gave us some of the run down on the guy, and he's a legend. Not only did he come up with the goods, but he paid his own way! If he's gone maverick...," Matt shuddered at the horrible possibilities, especially if the rumors about his time in Afghanistan were even half true. "Have you contacted Military intelligence?"

"Oh yes, the cavalry, as they say, is on the way. I've contacted headquarters, and we've gotten the green light on a sting."

"Frank, let's go carefully with this. I really think today is only a test run to see what she'd do. Somebody probably had her under surveillance the whole way, possibly the old master himself."

Frank shook his head in amazement, "The second pro you saw across the street. You may have been one of the few people alive to have seen Nicolai Androvich Gorgonov in action. Even so, she's trained to clear her path, obviously by the Shadow himself. She could have lost him. That could have been just a business man checking out her legs."

"You're not actually thinking of asking her to go through with it? If she meets them tomorrow, she's dead meat. You heard her. She hasn't practiced her craft in years. She buried it, man. She's rusty."

They went into Frank's office. Rusty and Jane were already seated at the conference table. "You've got someone watching, I assume?" Matt asked anxiously. Rusty and Jane nodded in unison as they continued studying the papers spread out on the table in front of them.

Frank addressed him from the other side of the table, "Step back and be objective, Matt," Frank's voice was tight. "This could be the big break in a major, devastating espionage ring. And who knows who this guy is feeding his information. With the contacts he made in Afghanistan, I shudder to think the damage he could do to our war on terror. For heaven's sake, Matt, this guy could be one of the few in the world who has the contacts to get to the core of Alkaida.

And what about the Russians or the Ukrainians? They're going to try to get ahead of us either in the machines of war or of commerce. Look at the Chinese. They've got the money now to buy the best information on the market and Gorgonov has the talent and connections to get the best. Not to mention organized crime. We've got enough problems with the Russian Mafia without letting them get an information and arms network going right under our noses. The Cartels have been hiring up ex-KGB talent like there's no tomorrow and its hurting our war on drugs more than anyone wants to admit. Nabbing this one operative, whatever his connections, could break open information highways in a number of directions depending on whether he's a maverick working for the highest bidder, or still somehow connected to one of the former Soviet republics.

Even so, I'm not advocating sacrificing this young woman. You know me better than that. I want you to go back in there and get details. Find out what she knows about how she got into the US in the first place. See what she's done to protect herself. And, Matt, don't ever forget that this could be a very clever run on the bureau. The other side wouldn't hesitate to sacrifice her to find out what we know and don't know about many things. She may or may not even know she's a sacrificial lamb. She also may be a very good actress. She wouldn't be the first beautiful woman to compromise American security." Frank turned to the other two agents, knowing he'd made his point with Matt.

Matt's heart was heavier as he made his way to again face "the little spook" as his colleagues had begun to call her. He realized how vulnerable he was. He'd been accepting her story without reservation. That wasn't like him at all. In fact, he'd begun to worry about how cynical he was becoming. Show him a pretty face, however, and he fell for anything. Disgusting. He didn't realize his determination was showing on his face until he stepped back into the interrogation room and saw fear flair for a moment in the blue eyes across from him. He trained his expression back to a business-like bland.

"You made sure no one followed you here?" he asked abruptly to get back to the business at hand.

"Yes, basically, I just followed my photo route. There's no way anyone can know from day to day where I'll go. I pick up new listings from realtors every day. No one knows how I'll work up my route. Most of my photos were in North Kitsap and Bainbridge Island today. It's very easy to get lost up there. It's practically impossible to follow someone without being noticed because of all the twists and turns and side roads. During the day, there's not much traffic in the residential areas, so I'd have noticed another car. The main problem was the ferry and the approach to it. To get here before 5:00, there's was only one I could have taken once I headed north. Someone could have been watching that. After the ferry docked in Seattle, I parked down by the Seattle Center and cleared my path all the way here. I snapped a couple of pictures of apartment buildings on the way here that one of my regular customers had expressed an interest in as investment property. I even took a quick tour through the Seattle Library to throw anyone off."

"Good." Matt responded and thought to himself they'd have her go back up the way she'd come if they could do it before the library closed. They could exit via the mail bay, and then it was just a block or so to the library. He took lunch hours there when he took one.

"I kept checking store fronts and all," she continued, "but I can't guarantee anything. My craft is rusty and, according to Peter, I was never very good."

"Perhaps that has an advantage. If you don't follow their rules, you'll be harder to track." Matt commented in an off-hand manner, his mind on the plans being formed in Frank's office.

Marta's heart chilled at the direction of their conversation. They were going to ask her to go through with it. She saw no hope that she would live through this. Silently praying to a God she knew little about, she acknowledged her fear. As if in answer to her cry, there was courage. A steel resolve formed within her. She knew this was right and she was going to do it, whatever they asked of her.

For the next hour, Matt took her through her story over and over again. She felt a sense of despair as she realized the agents might still not believe her. What would she do if they simply patted her on the head and sent her on her way as some kook or a lonely woman needing some attention? Her brain numbed as she went over the same ground, sometimes starting at one point, sometimes at another. She finally gave up all emotion and abandoned herself to the task of the present moment.

She was caught by surprise when Matt signaled the end of the interrogation with what she'd been taught was a closing question "Is there anything else you can think of that we should know?"

Her numbed brain could barely respond with a yes or a no, much less with any new information even if she'd had any. She managed to shake her head no. "Are you going to ask me to make contact?" She could restrain the anxious question no longer.

"I don't know yet," he answered noncommittally. "It's one consideration among many."

She nodded her understanding. He took the tape recorder and left her alone once more. Something she'd said had triggered major activity. She could feel it going on all around her. The very walls breathed quiet, effective action. She would join it eventually, even if it cost her life.

CHAPTER FOUR

Matt dropped the tape recorder off with the unit secretary as he hurried to Frank's office for the strategy meeting he knew was in progress. Jane and Rusty were still in the office with Frank. They all looked up from intense concentration as Matt entered.

Frank beamed at Matt. "Military intelligence is on the way to help beef up our manpower. It's a joint effort but we've got the lead. We'll field only FBI personnel for direct contact. The military will help with surveillance and back up. Everyone wants to know who's running this show and how big it is. Now, Matt, after going over Ms. Alexander's story, how high do you assess the risk to her?"

"The more she talked," Matt responded, "the better I liked it. She didn't exactly follow anyone's craft. She's developed her own though she doesn't think of it that way. She used the natural progression of her daily routine as an evasion technique. You've gone property hunting all over North Kitsap County with me, Frank. Do you think anyone could follow someone as familiar with it as she is through a completely unpredictable route without getting caught?"

Frank shook his head emphatically, his eyes sparkling with the shared memories he and Matt had of being hopelessly lost in some of the most beautiful scenery in the world.

"We still have to keep in mind that this could be a trick. Whoever activated her would stop her only if it was not their intention that she come here," Jane added quietly.

"Yes, a run on the agency is still within the realm of possibility," Frank agreed somberly.

"It's unlikely," Matt responded. "That's a suicide mission, and you don't usually find women involved with the factions who do that. If it's another covert agency, I would think getting her inside the agency rather than sending her in with a story this unlikely would be their goal. After all, she was born in the US. How far would we have checked beyond validating her birth certificate if she'd tried to get a job with the FBI? Think about it, put her in as clerical and she'd know most of what we doing here. Get her a college degree to go with her athleticism and we'd be recruiting her as an agent, probably would have offered her tuition while she worked for us."

"True enough," Rusty mused. "I started as a dark room tech and, when we went digital, the FBI paid for my degree to become an agent."

"It's happened," Jane countered. "Look at what the CIA's been going through. This could be an attempt to involve one or more of our agents in a scenario with a very beautiful woman. There are a multitude of possibilities for recruitment and compromise with a woman that beautiful and a story that paints her as the victim."

"I am having a hard time with that," Matt admitted candidly. "I'll have to entrust that to a better judge than I am. You guys keep me in prayer and keep a good eye on me." He grinned, knowing that each of the agents in the room would do exactly that.

Frank looked grim later that evening after he recapped the plan for the core team and briefed the support team. "It's time to get some sandwiches and coffee up here. Matt, get Ms. Alexander relaxed with some food, and then grill her one more time. Try to trip her up. We'll see if her story still tracks. What we've confirmed so far supports her story, but one more time can't hurt. Our military counterparts will be here within the hour, so let's get the situation locked down tight before they arrive. I want us ready to get into place tonight. Okay, everyone, get cracking."

Agents spread out to their various tasks. Matt gave his sandwich order and returned to the interrogation room.

Marta didn't know what she expected, but Matt's first question after more than an hour away wasn't it.

"What kind of sandwich would you like?" His tone was brisk, as if things were falling into place.

She realized that she was really hungry. "Turkey on wheat, please," she replied meekly.

"Decaf coffee again?"

"Yes, please."

He stuck his head out the door and gave her order to someone. "While we wait," he started conversationally, "tell me once more as much as you can about the workings of your KGB family." He put the little tape recorder back on the table and started it, so she knew his conversational tone belied his real purpose. They were checking out her story and then seeing if she changed anything to see if she'd been lying. She remembered this from Tanya's training. Always use as much of the truth as you can because lies are very hard to remember. Marta almost chuckled, but didn't. She was very glad she could tell the truth and not worry about remembering lies.

"Tanya always stressed not revealing the way the KGB works and keeping real names, traceable names, secret. For instance, I never knew Tanya or Peter's real names. I don't even know my own."

Matt nodded, encouraging her to continue. "Uncle Nicky was always a mystery to me. I never knew the rest of his name, just Nicky or Nicolai. No one ever seemed to know when he'd show up. I never knew where he came from except that he owned another tavern somewhere in the area. I always assumed he covered the Seattle area since Tanya and Peter seemed to cover Joint Base Lewis McChord."

Matt questioned her for another half an hour before a knock on the door told him the sandwiches had arrived. When he went out to get them, Jane signaled him to come all the way out. He closed the door.

"The military is here. I'm to take your place in there while you and Frank brief them. Then we're on our way to Kitsap County. Rusty snagged us an apartment right next to hers in Silverdale. Frank will give you the details. Your sandwich is in the conference room. Hurry, before somebody else grabs it," Jane grinned and carried their guest's sandwich in to the room with her own.

Marta watched as the lady put her food in front of her with a friendly grin, "Hi. I'm Jane and I'm hungry. How about you?" the agent gave a little chuckle. "I'm here to keep you company while conferences occur. Necessary evil." She shrugged expressively, and then bit ravenously into her own sandwich.

Marta felt a tremendous sense of relief at not having to eat with someone just sitting there watching her. As they ate, they made light conversation about the weather: when it had rained last, when it would rain again, and whether there would be another sparkling day of sunshine soon, each one considered the gold at the end of the rainbow in such wet country.

Marta realized this was just another interrogation technique, but it really didn't matter. She was actually very comfortable with this friendly person who seemed to believe her.

After they'd finished eating, the agent dropped her bomb, "How would you like a chance to prove whose side you're on?" The agent's eyes bored into hers.

Marta felt both panic and hope. They were going to ask her to go through with the meeting tomorrow. They were really going to take action on her situation. That meant they believed her story. She nodded her assent.

"Good," the agent, Jane, responded heartily, all business now as if Marta had just joined the right team and was getting her assignment on it. "What we want to do is draw out whoever used your KGB activation code by having you keep your appointment tomorrow while under FBI surveillance. Basically, do as they tell you, short of sabotage, assassination, or kidnapping. If they want you in a clandestine operation to gather information, we want you involved, and we'll follow your every move and record every contact. Agreed?"

"I agree," Marta said firmly, hoping her sheer terror didn't show up in her voice or body language.

"Okay, three of us will be moving in next door to you tonight. We will be a husband, wife and the wife's brother. We've come to the area to get in on some of the big construction jobs. The brother will become your new boyfriend. Will that cause any jealous current boyfriend to rush in and ruin the plan?"

"No, I don't date. I could never afford to let anyone get that close to me."

The agent quickly masked a brief flash of shock before she went on. "I'll be the wife, and you and I are to become really good neighbors. This is going to look like a major change in your life since you seem to have isolated yourself somewhat. The three of us will come on strong and very friendly. I'll have no problem playing the butt-insky motherly type – just comes natural to me." The agent grinned playfully and Marta thought this nightmare might have a few fun moments in it yet. "Matt will play a guy vying to be the new boyfriend. That should cover the major behavioral change if anyone's been watching you closely over the last few years. That's really about it for structure. A surveillance team will keep you covered at all times. The code word for help is 'peanut butter.'"

In the conference room, there were numerous uniforms present representing the Army, Navy, and Air Force. Frank delivered a curt, business-like briefing and then outlined the plan for a sting operation to draw out any hostile operatives.

"I'm sure you've noticed that elements of Marta Alexander's story directly relate to some of our current shared concerns. The link to a still active network of former KGB tavern owners is worth a reasonable risk."

"With one identified directly across from McChord," the Air force major interjected, "you'd better believe we think it's worth some risk to flush them out." The Navy and Army officers nodded their emphatic agreement with her statement.

"What about the lady in question? Has she agreed to your plan?" the Homeland Security representative asked.

"She's being offered the opportunity to cooperate as we speak. We have authorization from Washington to offer a chance at asylum. We'll have to see how she checks out, and then we'll approach immigration. If she is what she says she is and her help is valuable enough, we think there's a good chance for her to stay here and eventually become a citizen. We know there's a risk that this is an incredibly bold run on the agency. We might also have hit some nerves in the joint effort to investigate the tavern owner network that has been impacting information security around our troop deployments. She may be fishing for information or out to compromise the investigation in any way she can. Extreme care is definitely in order."

With that summary they moved on to hammer out an agreement as to what part each agency would play in the sting. The military agreed to provide heavy surveillance support since they had greater personnel resources. Homeland Security agreed to check out the identities, including Marta Alexander's, to see if they could trace how the "family" entered the US to begin with and how they set up their identities. The FBI would coordinate and actually execute the sting with their personnel. Frank introduced the scenario they'd already set and the two team members in the room. As if on cue, Jane joined them, explaining that another agent came in to give her an opportunity to brief them on her progress.

"I never made the asylum offer," Jane explained. "She agreed without conditions. Never even asked what was in it for her. We do have a problem, though." Matt felt his gut tighten as Frank gave a slight nod encouraging her to proceed. "She's lived in almost total isolation. She's never dated and has deflected overtures of friendship. She was afraid to let anyone close for fear of endangering them. We need an exceptional cover to get close to her. Any ideas?"

The room was ominously quiet. Evidently everyone was having the same problem Matt was having with the idea of a thirty-something beauty that'd never dated.

After a few uncomfortable seconds, Frank put them out of their misery, "I do have an idea. It's pretty wild so I want candid feed-back, especially from Matt, Jane and Rusty as the agents who'll be directly involved."

Matt literally tingled with anticipation as Frank took a deep breath. "The four of us who are assigned to direct contact with Ms. Alexander are Christians. It would not seem strange, especially to foreign intelligence operatives or to terrorist groups who've watched people literally give up their lives for their faith, that Marta's new neighbors would be aggressive in developing a close relationship with her to share their faith."

Matt sat up straighter in his chair, seeing not only a tremendous advantage for the current situation, but an incredible opportunity to share the Gospel with everyone involved in the operation and its surveillance, even the enemy.

"Won't that interfere with the boyfriend angle?" asked the Navy commander.

"No," Frank chuckled, "that's the beauty of it. Christian men fall in love with beautiful women, too, Commander. They just don't sleep with them until they're married. In the current culture, it would look unnatural for a sudden, strong attraction not to end in the bedroom very quickly unless there was some compelling reason to prevent it."

"Sounds plausible," the Army captain agreed. The Air Force major nodded her agreement with a secret smile that caused Matt to wonder if she were remembering some close encounters of her own or if she was a sister in Christ seeing all the possibilities.

"Do any of you object?" Frank turned his attention to Matt, Rusty, and Jane. Matt looked at the others. Rusty was openly grinning. Jane's eyes were twinkling with suppressed excitement. She nodded to Matt to be the spokesperson.

"No problem with us, Sir," he replied firmly.

"Very well, we have a plan. Let's do it." Frank gave a terse summary and made assignments. Matt, Rusty, and Jane left to make their way to Kitsap County.

Marta tensed to fight or flee as a ragged man approached her when she neared the Seattle Center where her car was parked. He only wanted money and looked like he needed it. She noticed a woman and child hovering in the background. Watching her surroundings vigilantly, she bought herself some surveillance time by digging out a ten-dollar bill and stuffing it into his hand before she moved any closer to her car. She registered the surprised tears in his eyes only as a way to remember the face if she saw it again.

Marta then kept moving relentlessly on through the Seattle Center, pausing casually to look at the Center House and take a survey of faces behind her. Then she continued onward into the dangerous, murky night.

Nicolai Androvich had ample opportunity for thought as he watched Marta's beat up VW bug. He hadn't bothered keeping an eye on the Federal Building. There were two major and several minor exits but only one of him. He knew she would come back to her car. Knowing her was his only advantage in this dangerous game. All he knew of the kingpin of the network of renegade former KGB agents and power mad gangsters was the code name "Shatoon." This keyed him into the Ukrainian connection because it was the name of the vicious renegade bears so feared in the Ukraine. It was almost as if the name was a direct taunt at Nicolai.

Nicolai shook away the superfluous thoughts. If the Shatoon's network had other surveillance on Marta, they'd have to watch all exits from the Federal Building. Hopefully that would keep them too busy to mess with her car. He had no intention of losing her to a car bomb…or to any other nasty surprise the Shatoon might have laid out.

Nicolai sighed as he enjoyed his veritable invisibility in the new world order. When the Soviet Union fell, he'd simply disappeared into his own network of an underground free enterprise he'd built under the Communists' very noses. He was now one of the few entrepreneurs in the former Soviet Union completely free of organized crime ties. He had no ties to them because they were afraid of him. It was lovely, simply lovely. They'd soon learned, when they tried to strong arm his business associates that they were former KGB and Spetsnatz trained operatives who wanted no criminal associations. They wanted their country's freedom and to do business in a free enterprise system.

The risks had been terrible. He'd earned his legendary status in the Spetsnatz and then the KGB with unusual plans that bore a plentiful harvest of information without revealing to the source that they'd compromised security. That was the beauty of his method, he chuckled to himself. Bits and pieces of information from a multitude of sources mixed with an active imagination gave him the best information in the business. Of course, he had taken incredible risks. He always knew that, eventually, his little game could catch up with him. Fortunately for him, the Soviet Union crumbled in on itself before someone did something totally unpredictable and revealed him for the fraud he was. Yes, most of his information was clever fiction.

In this case, however, he was back to taking terrible risks. Marta could be the one to do something totally unpredictable. Her method for clearing her path was surely unique. Nicolai chuckled again. Then brought himself up sharp. He couldn't blunt his awareness. If there was a Shatooni tail, he would spot it as his daughter approached her car. So far, no attempt had been made to tamper with it. He'd taken the risk of checking it out for bugs and bombs. His own car was parked within easy range of his surveillance. He could not only guard it but get to it quickly to follow Marta when she came. Then again, he might be in the cross hairs of an assassin's rifle now.

Actually, if it weren't for his daughter and her safety, Nicolai wouldn't mind such an easy death. A quick bullet to the back of the head was not such a bad way to go. It didn't look like his dream of a farm where he could grow food to feed hungry Ukrainians was ever going to happen. He'd dreamed of making a government that supported the farmers and shop keepers and truck drivers and railroad workers. He'd done much to make that happen. His small group of hand-picked agents had been carefully trained in the ways of entrepreneurship and the free market system. They had taken classes at the University of Washington in everything from agriculture to software engineering. That was the most valuable information Nicolai had sent home, not American technology of war, but their technology of commerce.

How is it possible to become the bread basket of the world? Any student of history knows that is where the power lies. Everyone has to eat. There has to be enough water and land and life giving seed to feed people. The trusted few in his secret network had studied the best in agriculture, animal husbandry, environmental management and business management in the current bread basket of the world. His dream was that the Ukraine would become the next bread basket of the world, not only able to feed her own people, but the rest of the world as well.

Of course, the way Americans were selling farm land to foreign interests, the Ukraine might have to feed Americans, too in the next century. Americans were so naïve. They were so worried about their technology but sold the very ground under their feet to those who cared nothing for the welfare of American children. Pah! Such thinking. It was as bad as Moscow.

Nicolai hadn't missed his chance, though. He owned a good chunk of American soil, too. Much of the produce of that soil went to the care and feeding of Ukrainians, much to the dismay of the "Mafia" bosses. They had found an entirely unexpected situation in trying to intimidate his people. They had found trained soldiers armed with an arsenal. They had found hardened warriors in the field of international espionage trained in every aspect of clandestine operations and covert combat. After all, you can't fight an enemy you can't find and who knows more about your operations than you do.

He funded his network well from a series of Swiss Bank Accounts. America had been good to them. Nicolai and his group had come and earned all they needed simply by entering into the market place and applying all the rules the Americans seemed to have forgotten. All the while, Nicolai sent home nonsense that pleased his KGB "masters" immensely.

If he believed in God, he would call it a miracle. If Anna had lived, he might believe in the loving God all the Christians talked about. No, he mustn't think of her.

He caught a movement out of the corner of his eye and watched as Anna's daughter approached her VW with the caution of one whom he had personally trained. She had her mother's face and eyes…ivory and blue fire. She moved with her mother's grace, but luckily, she had his power and at least some of his height. She also had his skills. They would both need all those skills now. Thoughts of her mother would only blunt his keenness with anguish.

Marta was approaching her car. This was the most dangerous part. If enemies were watching, and surely they were, they would have the car under surveillance. If they had seen her go into the Federal Building, they'd just kill her, and there were a million ways to do that. He watched as she cautiously studied her car as she came closer. She bent down and checked the undercarriage. She seemed to hold her breath as she slid her hand under the hood and the trunk checking for trip wires. Then she cautiously opened the door, poised to run should there be a tell-tale click. She threw her purse on the driver's seat, then got in and checked under the steering column and the glove box. He followed along the check list he'd taught her and sighed with relief when she switched on the engine. All the classic detonator points were past. Behold, she lived. Perhaps there was a God after all.

Matt drove into the carport under their new apartment in Silverdale. The assistant manager had been alerted and was waiting for them with a key. The three agents then moved quietly and efficiently to bring in the few boxes and suitcases that held their meager personal items and masked the plethora of portable surveillance equipment disguised in moving boxes. They knew a van had moved into place earlier to monitor the area and to do a sweep for other active surveillance equipment. The "all-clear" had been sounded. Matt couldn't help but think it was strange. Whoever had activated her should be monitoring her. Why weren't they? Or had something been missed? Had something been developed that US equipment couldn't pick up? Matt made a mental note to have military intelligence check it out. Maybe the CIA had updated information on new surveillance technology. It was tough to keep up with information age spy-ware these days. He then put the worry before the throne of God in prayer and continued with the business of setting up a surveillance station and cover story.

Jane casually left her overnight case in the car so that Matt would have an excuse to run downstairs as soon as their monitor showed the subject was approaching. Ms. Alexander had been given a homing device for her car and one for her person. He sincerely hoped that their technology exceeded those of their hidden enemy so they wouldn't pick up the signals.

The plan was that Matt would "run into" Marta as she arrived so they could strike up an immediate acquaintance. Matt was checking out the couch in the living room when the monitor indicated that Marta's car was within range. The three agents went on high alert as her car approached the apartment complex. They heard her car pull in, and Matt went into action.

Marta pulled her camera and route slips together slowly. She wanted to give the agents plenty of time to get down from the apartments above to the car ports so they could bump into each other. As she got out of the car, she saw Matt approaching. Her heart did a little flip-flop. She ignored it and prepared to respond to his lead.

"Well, hi," his deep masculine voice warmed her with its friendliness, and she found herself wishing it was real. "It looks like we're going to be neighbors." He indicated their adjoining parking slots and continued smiling at her as he got a little case from the front seat of the car next to hers.

She had to respond somehow, but her mind was a frozen blank.

"Can I help you carry anything?" He helped her with the perfect opening.

"Thanks, but no. I just have my camera and route sheets."

"Nice camera. Are you a professional photographer?"

"In a way. I take pictures of houses for local realtors and multiple listing services."

Jane appeared at the top of the stairs. "Matt, what's taking you so long? Oh, hello," she grinned broadly. "Leave it to my brother to meet a pretty girl in the first five minutes in a new place."

Marta blushed and laughed off the remark.

"We're just moving in as you can see. Sure lucked out getting this place on such short notice. It was nothing short of a miracle. Name's Jane O'Hara." She stuck out her hand so Marta transferred her route sheets and maps to her left hand so she could shake hands.

"My name's Marta Alexander, and if yours is the open doorway, my apartment is the one just past it."

"Great! In a house full of men, it's nice to have a female neighbor. I have both my husband and my little brother. Men! You can't live with 'em and you can't kill 'em," Jane laughed merrily. "Well, we'll let you get to your place. You look like you're just getting home from a long day. Come over for coffee in the morning around 6:30 or 7:00 if you're up. Matt usually runs at 5:00, so we breakfast after that. We can get acquainted then."

"Oh, I usually run at 5:00, too." Marta forgot her role for a moment in the warmth of the possibility that this disturbing but attractive man might join her in her morning run.

Matt's face lit up, "I'll see you first thing in the morning then. You can show me the best places to run."

At that point, Rusty stepped out of the open door. "First I lose one worker, now I lose the worker I sent searching. What's going on out here?"

"Rusty, meet our neighbor. I'm terrible with names, Marta was it?" Marta nodded her assent as the friendly Jane gave her a sheepish look. "Marta, this is my husband, Rusty." They shook on the introduction. "She's going to run with Matt and then have breakfast with us tomorrow."

"Wonderful! It will even out the odds. My wife feels a little outnumbered at our place, so it's nice to have a close neighbor to share 'girl stuff' with." He wiggled his eyebrows up and down in such a fantastic expression that Marta couldn't hold back a laugh.

Nicolai nodded to his long-time friend Tanya who had been monitoring the action from his watch post in the apartment directly across from Marta's. He bought the entire complex several years ago. He had secreted away enough cash to make it a practically untraceable transaction through one of his many corporate accounts. It had been a risk, setting up a hiding place across from Marta, but if everything blew up, he wanted to be able to quickly pick her up and take her to another refuge. No matter what the cost to himself, he would protect Marta.

He knew she was not safe now that the Shatooni were operating nearby. They knew who she was and they could destroy her. They had to be stopped. Nicolai snorted at the unholy alliance these former colleagues of his had made with the powerful drug cartels and the terrorists operating from too many covert hiding places all over the world.

When he finally stopped them, at least this little cadre of them, and when he finally had Marta safe, he would go home. He would feel the deep, rich earth of that family farm once more before he died. He hoped to be buried on that farm where the bones of his ancestors had rested for centuries. Those names had been carefully printed in his grandmother's Bible. Her Bible was the reason his grandmother's bones did not lie within the welcome warmth of the family farm, but lay instead in the frozen waste of Siberia.

He had never understood why the Bible was important enough to his grandmother that she would die for it, but because it was he kept it secreted away. A broken and scarred man had stopped by one day when he was still a small boy and left her Bible with him, whispering for him to take great care with it. He would give it to Marta one day. He wanted her to know the depths of Ukrainian sorrow, the depths of the Ukrainian soul. This was her heritage.

CHAPTER FIVE

Marta awoke just before her alarm went off with a sense of anticipation. Something was different. She heard the stirring in the next apartment and remembered. Caught between a delicious sense of not being alone anymore and a horrible sense of danger, she got ready for her morning run. Matt greeted her with a big grin as she came out of her apartment and delicious won out.

"Great morning, huh?" he asked. "It's only raining a little."

Marta laughed as she used the railing to stretch. Matt let her set the pace as they took off along the Silverdale waterfront route, passing a mixture of glitzy new and quaint old homes and businesses. Not until they were running through the business district by the mall where the early morning traffic noise would cover their conversation did they begin to speak. Matt briefed her as they ran.

"Your instructions were to take the 4 p.m. ferry from Bremerton to Seattle, right?" She nodded affirmatively. "Okay, if you're not contacted on the ferry, you're to go toward the waterfront park and wait there. We'll have people with you the whole way but don't look for them. We don't want to tip anyone off. You can bet the other side will be watching you this trip. If it goes sour, hit the ground and roll away from the contact. The cavalry will take it from there. Any questions?"

"Yes, getting to the ferry, will I be going about my normal business? I have most of yesterday's photo route to finish. Following me could be pretty tricky."

"We'll take a copy of your photo slips at breakfast. We have a very quiet photo copier set up in the apartment. We'll pass the copies on to the surveillance crew."

"Be sure to keep them in the exact order I give them to you in. That will be how I've routed myself out."

"Will do," he smiled. "Any other questions?" She shook her head no. "Good! I'll race you back!" Matt took off with a devilish grin. Marta kicked into stride and caught up to him. One thing her KGB mom had given her was world-class athletic training and no mere FBI agent was going to beat her in a foot race.

"Nicolai, do you think they saw me?" a breathless blond asked anxiously as they watched their targets race head to head toward Marta's apartment complex from Nicolai's window.

"No, she'd have reacted somehow. She's had training but no real practice, no real discipline. You trained her well, Tanya, but only field experience with lives on the line develops the absolute control that overcomes a shock such as seeing your 'mother' where you didn't expect her after years of silence."

"They've gone into the FBI apartment," Tanya observed. "How sure are you this place is clean?"

"I just swept it. They have a van down there to the right." He pointed to a buff-colored van with what looked like an advertisement for a plumbing outfit on the side. "It probably has a directional mike in it."

Tanya nodded when she saw it. "We'll have to be careful with that activated." Their recording device had kicked on at the first noise from Marta's apartment. Their technology was based on Nicolai's own design, using a satellite owned by one of his corporations. So far, to the best of their knowledge, no one else could track it. Their device picked up Matt and Marta's entry back into the FBI apartment. There was general greeting and morning chatter accompanied by the clatter of dishes. Then there was quiet. That got the two former KGB agent's attention. Too much quiet could mean trouble.

"Our dear Heavenly Father," Rusty prayed as Matt on one side of Marta and Jane on the other took one of her hands and bowed their heads. Marta quickly followed suit, unsure of what to do. She waited for her cue as Rusty continued. "We thank You for Your abundant care for us. You've given us a roof over our heads, food on our table, each other to share our lives, and Your precious Son as a redeeming sacrifice for our sin so You could even give us Yourself in our hearts and lives. Your presence with us is a treasure beyond price. Your care is all-powerful and omniscient. There is no other God beside You. Nothing escapes Your loving concern. Be with each of us today as we go out into the world. Protect us. Thank You for our new friend Marta. We ask Your special blessing and protection on her this day. In Christ's Name we pray, amen."

Matt and Jane each murmured "Amen" and squeezed Marta's hand. By instinctive reaction, she squeezed back, unsure of the meaning of the gesture. When she looked up, Jane was passing the scrambled eggs. The chatter started again as if nothing awesome had happened. Marta followed their lead, wondering if the last few seconds had simply been part of their cover or if they were genuine in what they said.

Matt quietly got up and started copying the route sheets that she had quickly ducked into her apartment to get. He got them started and came back to eat, joining in the merry banter Rusty and Jane kept up.

"If you'd caught that pop fly, we would have won that game, Rusty," Matt groused as he sat down.

"Nonsense," he countered. "You pitched it right to him. That batter couldn't have missed it if he'd tried."

"Says you!" And on it went, clear through the breakfast dishes, which Jane and Matt did because Rusty had cooked. When Marta protested, Jane informed her that tomorrow would be her day to cook, but today she was still a guest. For the first time in her life, Marta felt a sense of belonging. This is what a family was supposed to look like.

Then it hit her: this wasn't a real family. They were playacting before a hostile audience. Her dark thoughts were suddenly interrupted by a comment from Rusty.

"We take time for family devotions each morning before we start our day," Rusty smiled as he brought a worn Bible to the breakfast table after the dishes had been merrily done, covering the sound of the copy machine that had now finished. "We have a Christian home and want to be sure our Lord goes with us in all things so we can introduce Him to everyone we meet. We set aside a special time for Him each morning. We'd love to have you join us, but if you'd rather go on about your day, we won't hold you."

Marta was fascinated. She didn't know if this was part of the cover or not, but she'd obviously been given permission to participate if she wanted. She chose to stay. "I'd like to stay if you don't mind. Just tell me what to do or not do so I don't intrude."

Jane leaned over and hugged her, "You couldn't intrude if you tried. You're more than welcome with us." Jane's warmth and sincerity almost brought tears to her eyes. This feeling of belonging was too fresh and rare to give up, even for a second. She just nodded, not trusting herself to speak.

Rusty read several verses from the Bible: one about going in the strength you have and another about a boy giving some bread and fish to Jesus. That one loaf of bread and one fish fed a whole crowd of people. Marta had never heard of such a thing. It caught her imagination in a way nothing else ever had.

They each prayed aloud but no one seemed to expect that of Marta, so she just tucked her head down and waited for the "amen." They sang a short song about God being glorified in a bunch of different ways and then Rusty stretched, obviously ending the session.

One more as yet undetected presence signaled his network to begin closing in on the one young woman who was the key to it all. Code name Shatoon had listened in cold rage to the fanatics who would force their concept of God on others. He cursed their pernicious timing. These interfering, insistent, incessant Christians could ruin his plan if they got too close. No! These bumbling, mindless fanatics would not get in his way. If they got close, he'd simply eliminate them. A nice drive-by shooting, perhaps? Who would notice in the carnage of America these days?

He took pleasure in his rage, not questioning its source, instead focusing it on his plan to gain power, prestige, and revenge. His network would follow this woman. He would gain control of Nicolai's vast resources, and he would make him beg for death in his suffering, leaving him empty of hope as he, the Shatoon, had been left when Anna died. Anna had been his everything. He had even loved her enough to give her to the one she thought she loved more than him. That monster Nicolai had killed her.

Nicolai watched his treasure so closely it would take much to get her from him. But the crafty master spy had made his first mistake. Tanya had inadvertently led his enemy right to his door and revealed his secret Achilles heel…the daughter who had taken Anna from him in the rigors of her birth. With the information he'd carefully fed Tanya, he knew that Nicolai would have to act. Just as the Shatoon had hoped, Nicolai had used his last untainted resource…his daughter. She could approach the FBI for him and make sure the information reached them before it was too late.

Only Nicolai had known the daughter's recognition code. Only Nicolai could activate her. Now that he had, she was out in the open and anyone's game. It would not be Nicolai's operative that she would meet in Seattle today. It would be the Shatoon's. All the years of keeping tabs on the legendary Shadow Man had paid off. The timing couldn't be more perfect with his new partners pressuring him for action. Nicolai's operative wouldn't dare show her face. Sweet Marta would then become a pawn in his own network to bring down those who stood in his way in Washington, D.C. Those "do-gooders" who kept their attention and resources focused on his little corner of the world, interfering with his business and wrecking havoc on his profits. Once they were sent packing with their tails between their legs, he, the Shatoon, would devour both father and daughter.

If those fanatics who moved in next to the daughter poisoned her mind against obedience, he would eradicate them. It used to be, at home, one phone call would have spirited such people away to a mental hospital or work camp. Not any more! They were free to spread their poison while he was not free to go home. The secrets that had once been protected in the KGB vaults were now floating all over the place. The opportunists who'd broken in and stolen them were even selling them to the corrupt capitalists in Hollywood. His power and position had been stripped from him at home. He would be a pariah, perhaps even find himself in one of the camps or prisons to which he had sent many others.

But he had been wise and had made, long ago, other arrangements for himself and his private network. Old friends had welcomed him back in some of his former haunts. Even that was now in peril because of a stubborn senator and his equally obtuse aid that were determined to cut off the flow of drugs to America thus the funding pipe line of the old friends who were making the Shatoon rich. The aid had a weakness, though, for lovely young women, and the beautiful Marta was just the one to exploit that weakness.

Marta returned to her apartment, grabbed her camera to go with her route sheets, and headed for her classic VW. She saw Rusty, under the guise of heading to work, drop a set of duplicate route sheets at a predetermined drop for pick-up by a secondary military surveillance van. She knew he would then head in to the Seattle office to reconnoiter with Frank.

Jane would remain at the apartment and monitor Marta's apartment and the immediate area for activity. A military police unit was within striking distance if she called for backup.

Matt had his own set of duplicate route sheets and would rendezvous with the primary surveillance team in the FBI van.

Matt swung into the front passenger seat and began giving directions from the route sheets.

"I have contact with the target," came a crisp, business-like voice from the back of the van. Matt spotted her at once as she snapped her picture, jumped back in the VW, and headed to the next site. So it would go until she had to catch the 4:00 ferry from downtown Bremerton to Seattle. With the Naval Shipyard traffic and commuters returning from Seattle, it would be a madhouse downtown. Whoever had chosen the contact environment had chosen well. It would be easy to get lost in the crowd and make surveillance next to impossible. Matt took comfort in the thought that once on the ferry, no other changes could occur. It was probable, however, that the contact would be made on the other side in the teeming crowd of the Seattle waterfront. The crowds would be at their peak when the ferry docked on the other side.

The rest of the day would have been simply boring if Matt hadn't felt the tension of the upcoming meeting. Marta would be in her greatest known danger during the actual contact. Although they hadn't picked up any sign of other surveillance, Matt knew there had to be something out there. This could be a low budget operation with its own completely unpredictable agenda. The thought made Matt's blood run cold. At least with one of the major players there was some sort of predictable craft. With a small, maverick operation, nobody knew what to expect. No, he decided, this had to have some tie to the former KGB and its craft. They knew Marta's recognition code – if Marta was telling the truth.

Marta had almost forgotten the significance of the day in the routine of her photo route. Then she noticed the time. It was almost 3:00, and her route was taking her into downtown Bremerton. She still had plenty of time to finish her route, find a parking spot, and make the 4:00 ferry. Her photos were now of older homes, some picturesque and quaint, some spectacular, others just run down and old. She'd always been fascinated with the homes around the Naval Shipyard, wondering how old they were and what the town had looked like in the late nineteenth century when the Shipyard was first built. She forced her concentration back on getting through the heavy traffic to one of the crowded parking areas near the ferry dock. Waiting at a light, she noticed a buff-colored van pulling up just behind her in her lane. She thought she recognized Matt.

"Surely he won't follow me on the ferry," she thought in alarm. "That would be stretching coincidence a bit too far." By the time she looked back again, the guy who looked like Matt had disappeared, and someone else, a blond guy, was at shot gun.

Matt quickly changed places with Bill as they drew up behind Marta to ensure no one would catch a glimpse of him as they approached the contact environment. The military would take over now, and Matt felt a terrible sense of loss as they watched Marta pull into a parking lot. If all went well, he would see her back at the apartment tonight. If all did not go well, he might never see her alive again. He began to pray with a fervency that surprised him. In a very short time, he had come to care deeply for this seemingly vulnerable young woman. He had to remember that she could be a vicious enemy determined to destroy him and everything he held dear. He prayed for the Lord's protection for both of them. Even if she was an enemy, it was scriptural for him to pray blessings for her and for his own tottering heart.

Marta finished her business in the parking lot and hurried with the crowd to catch the Bremerton Ferry to Seattle. Once the ferry was underway, she found a seat and waited tensely. She didn't really expect to be contacted on the ferry because there were no escape routes, but it was a possibility.

The beautiful scenes of water, trees, homes with beautifully manicured lawns, the Seattle skyline, and towering mountains that usually enthralled Marta were lost on her now. Finally they reached the Coleman dock in downtown Seattle. She joined the crowd slowly moving toward the ramp connecting them with the dock. As she inched along, she was suddenly aware of a presence close behind her.

"Don't look around," whispered the very familiar rasping voice of her KGB "father." She kept walking as if she hadn't heard, feeling that malevolent presence. Chills were running down her spine. This was a man who had frightened her from her earliest memory. There was no sense of the comforting presence of Tanya, her KGB "mother." Always it had been Tanya who had stood between the frightened child and this cold, sinister man. Marta realized now that Tanya had been her fierce protector, made clear by her very absence. Later Uncle Nicky had added an even more powerful protective layer around her. There was no one to shield her now. Suddenly the prayers of the morning came to her mind. The God that Matt, Jane, and Rusty had prayed to could perhaps be a shield. They'd asked His protection for her this morning. Marta would appeal to their God.

"Sir," she silently sent her thoughts upward, "I've always been told that You aren't there, but if You are, could you please help me? I realize I'm not qualified for Your help, but Matt and Rusty and Jane seem to know you rather well and to think that You care about people. Anyway, they said you sent Your Son for some reason, so maybe because of that I can qualify to talk to You. I sure hope so, because I really need Your help right now."

She walked in front of her terrifying captor until they reached the street level from the second story ferry exit ramp. "Turn left," he hissed behind her.

They walked past the busy shops, restaurants, and amusements of the lively waterfront until they came to a concrete and orange railing park. Marta felt intense relief that Peter had chosen the very spot Matt had told her to head for if she could. This park had not trees or grass, just concrete and orange railings. She'd always thought park was a misnomer. What a ridiculous thought to be having at such a time. She thought of her beloved park in Silverdale and wondered if she'd live to see it again.

They stopped at a railing where they stood looking out over the panoramic view of the Puget Sound and the majestic Olympic mountains beyond. Her thoughts turned to her unseen audience. There was some comfort in knowing that Peter had walked into a trap.

"My dear daughter," Peter's voice dripped with sarcasm, "what a touching reunion for us, eh?" He laughed cruelly, sending spasms through Marta's already tense body. How often she had heard and hated that laugh while she was growing up. Always he had taunted her for her stupidity and failure to please. Always there had been vicious reminders that she was in his power. In the past, Tanya or Uncle Nicky had stood between them. Neither was here now, yet she felt a protective presence. A strange peace descended on her. She wondered if Matt's God was answering her prayer.

Peter rudely interrupted her wanderings, "You are about to repay Mother Russia for all the care she has taken of you, my dear." A few rather nasty responses occurred to Marta, but she wisely kept them to herself. "We have a job for you. His name is Timothy Parsons and he's a rather talented young aid to a powerful Senator. He's also the spoiled son of another powerful man with, shall we say, connections to the Pentagon. We'd like you to attract this man to your lovely self and wrap his heart strings around your little finger. Once you've accomplished this task, which should be relatively easy for someone with your...assets," he paused significantly as he ran his eyes over her entire body in a most un-fatherly fashion, "we'll determine the most appropriate control on Parsons.

He will be here over the next few weeks for a visit to hearth and home, a touching sentimental journey he makes to his mother who no longer has any sentimental attachment to his father. When at home, he mostly parties with his pals but his crowning glory is running in the Whaling Days race." Peter rolled his eyes with obvious disgust at this silly pastime. "A perfect assignment for you, is it not? Perfectly suited for what little you have to offer: mindless running and…well, need I say more?" Peter's suggestive tone made her skin crawl.

All business now, Peter continued, "You have exactly two weeks to secure his undying affection or at least compromise him beyond all hope or cure to place him permanently under my thumb. He arrives tomorrow and his invariable pattern is to run in, kiss Mama, and immediately repair to his favorite watering hole with his rowdy friends. Such filial devotion warms ones heart, does it not?

All you need to do is show up at this watering hole. If he runs true to form, he'll take care of the rest. We'll get it all on camera and decide where to go from there. I have the utmost confidence in your success, Lovely One, because it would be most unpleasant, most unpleasant indeed, for you if you fail. Am I understood?"

He crooned the last in such a poisonous tone that Marta's stomach lurched with nausea. She swallowed several times to keep from being sick and nodded, indicating she understood only too well.

He seemed to enjoy her discomfort as he continued, "I should also remind you that there is no Uncle Nicky or Mama Tanya to whine to now. At last I heard, they were recalled to Moscow in disgrace when the Soviet government fell. It seems certain files came to light with their names connected with nefarious activities the new government quite frowned upon. Tsk, tsk, the people of the new government were ever so upset with them. Who knows, your success in this mission may improve whatever miserable conditions they've been enduring ever since. Of course, there is no guarantee they are even still alive, I'm just saying.... Isn't it fortunate that some farsighted people saw fit to do a little strategic file removal before that fateful storming of our beloved KGB headquarters? Of course, anything anyone really needed to know was left directly in their path."

Marta was appalled! Was it true? Had the former KGB had time to remove files and only leave ones they wanted found? Had they perhaps even replaced true files with falsified ones? She remembered watching it on TV. It seemed so long ago now that having it affect her was surreal. What a disinformation coup it would be if the KGB actually pulled it off. She should warn someone. Then she remembered that the FBI was recording every word. She almost chuckled at the irony. Here Peter had taken all that trouble to protect himself but was signing his own arrest warrant by bragging about it to her.

Tanya watched the nondescript van across the street, knowing the conversation was being recorded by high tech audio equipment. The surrounding noise would be filtered out by the computer, leaving only the two voice signatures in the target conversation. Marta Alexander's voice signature would already have been programmed in from the FBI interrogation tapes to provide an anchor for the directional mike.

A "casual tourist" with a telephoto lens was recording every nuance of facial expression on the target and her contact. It was apparent that the contact was totally unaware of any surveillance presence. Tanya shook her head as she observed the full force of the American surveillance recording the wrong conversation. How had the Shatoon hijacked Nicolai's operation? She didn't dare try to find Nicolai from her position for fear she'd tip the FBI to her presence. She was unsure how to proceed, so she continued to record with her own masked directional.

"So, you have your task, Marta," all the high tech equipment recorded the cold voice as it continued. "The man of your dreams will be at the Silverdale Tavern tomorrow night. You will show an intense interest in him and overwhelm him with your beauty. Once he's in your power, we'll give you further instructions. And, please, fix yourself up a bit: nice clothing, get your hair done, a little make up." The casual tourist's camera recorded him handing her a fat package.

Tanya thought that Marta must be in shock, she moved so slowly as she took the envelope. Peter continued his verbal torture, "This should help. It's nice, freshly laundered money. That's one thing the old geezer Nicky taught me, never under-fund an operation. Well, my dear 'daughter,' don't say your loving 'papa' never gave you anything. Ta, ta." His mirthless laugh echoed and he left the scene. Tanya could tell from Marta's pallor that her stomach was heaving. The poor thing had always had a sensitive stomach. Strangely though, Tanya sensed a peace in her that she'd never had before. Perhaps the prayers they'd heard this morning were not such nonsense after all. Anything that would bring a little peace to this mess couldn't be all bad.

CHAPTER SIX

Nicolai watched in dismay as his contact with Marta was snatched away from him by one of the very men he was out to stop. This rogue agent wanted and hunted as the vicious criminal he was, stepped right in and intercepted his contact. Somehow, someone had tracked the Shadow Man. His craft was compromised. It was all the protection he'd ever had, and it had been stripped away from him in seconds. Worse, it could not be this one who had cracked it. He was too stupid. There must be another somewhere, watching him even now. And Marta was utterly exposed.

He caught sight of the nondescript van out of the corner of his eye. Did they know of this also? Yet as he listened to the pig Petrov taunt Marta mercilessly, he concluded that at least the swine didn't know. His elaborate lying gave away that some-one knew strategic files were missing. Someone knew he or Tanya or both had them. Someone knew of his connection with Marta. That was the key. Only a few people knew that Marta was his daughter.

He watched Petrov break contact with Marta and move off. Marta headed back for the ferry. Nicolai's heart wrenched at her paleness. This would be torture for the naïve, innocent girl. He had protected her from the kind of the training Petrov thought she'd had. He had intervened with the help of Tanya who had not been spared the most devastating and demeaning "training" the KGB forced on the young women it recruited. It amounted to nothing less than prostitution and violated a woman's deepest and most tender feelings. Of all that he hated about the KGB, that training ranked right up there with taking orphans and making sleeper spies out of them. How he wished he had been there to help topple the statue of Lenin and rip open the KGB records during his homelands successful fight to end Communism. He could have given the people a nice tour. Petrov was bluffing about pulling out strategic records. Nicolai knew who had been there, and they had brought him the treasure trove of records. Treating people decently did sometimes pay off.

He watched as Tanya made her surreptitious way toward the ferry following Marta. Hers was the most dangerous job now, for she was known to both the girl and her contact. Tanya was, however, the mistress of disguise. After all, she'd been taught by the master, or former master. He didn't know if he would have recognized her if he hadn't known where to look. How, he wondered, did she make herself look so much shorter? Yet, her stride was a bit too athletic for the role of crippled old woman she was now playing. He would have to pass that on. It might save her life some day. Always the teacher, Nicolai chided himself.

The *Shatoon*'s cold gray eyes watched the hated Gorgonov from a store just behind the parking area where the van sat. As he watched the old veteran, the "master spy" of the KGB, he reflected on his theory that Gorgonov had gotten away with a lot because of his mystique. He had been nicknamed "The Shadow Man" in Spetsnatz because he could just disappear. He could blend into any group and make people so comfortable that they would discuss almost anything with him. The KGB had been so interested in mastering his craft; they had actively recruited him and, after one supposedly failed attempt to break his craft, simply overlooked the fact that he could use it to evade their controls. He made them his slaves by producing such brilliant intelligence coups. Although he sometimes simply disappeared, he always came back with the information they needed, always.

Revenge was close. How appropriate that Anna's daughter should be the means. His new friends in Mexico would enjoy her.

Or perhaps he'd barter her to the less religious of his contacts in Afghanistan. Oh, yes, he would keep her alive. She was the key to controlling the mighty Gorgonov.

Marta made it to the ferry terminal ladies room before the nausea completely overcame her, but it was a close call. She got cleaned up, bought her ticket, and took time to compose herself before the next ferry to Bremerton pulled out. She made the rest of the trip to Silverdale in a fog of physical illness, but that strange peace stayed with her. She clung to it and to the idea that Matt would be there. And he was. She hadn't made it to the first stair before he was greeting her.

"Here's my running partner," he studied her face a second then offered his arm. "You look a little green around the gills, Kid. Did I run you into the ground this morning?"

He made the last sound like a joke, but she sensed real concern in the way he was holding her up. She just leaned against him as he half carried her up the stairs. He pulled her into his apartment, and she rushed straight to the bathroom. Matt held her head while she wretched. He put her on the couch, brought her 7-UP, and held the glass to her lips when her shaking fingers wouldn't work. She sipped carefully, swallowed tentatively. It stayed down. She leaned toward the strength next to her, and Matt pulled her into his strong embrace. His kindness was too much for her, and the tears came silently. Marta had never in her life had the privilege of crying out loud.

Matt looked up as Jane and Rusty clattered in and came to a dead stop. "Hi guys," Matt said from the couch. "Looks like our neighbor picked up a touch of the flu, or our breakfast didn't agree with her." He tried to throw a little levity into the situation. "Don't worry, though, I'll clean up the bathroom."

"Don't be gross," Jane reproved in a jocular tone that did not match the deep concern in her eyes. She went to the girl silently sobbing in Matt's arms. She wisely took over the comforting duties, giving Matt a stern look as he reluctantly let go of her.

He knew he was in for a lecture, but he didn't care. That girl had been broken today. He didn't know why or how, but considering the strength she had shown thus far in her strange life, the final blow must have been beyond devastating. Even yet, she retained silence to protect their cover.

Matt watched helplessly as Jane held the girl and rubbed her back until the tears ran dry. Rusty took up the cover chatter, indicating that his cooking had been insulted and his revenge would be dinner. He began clattering pots and pans to cover the drama taking place in the living room. Too much silence made for too much curiosity from a surveillance team.

Marta looked up and took the tissues Matt offered. He saw the courage and color return to her face and felt a swelling in his heart. She was an extraordinary woman.

"Oh, I'm all right now," she said in a bright but brittle voice. "I had to go to Seattle today on business. I always stuff myself on those waffle ice cream cones with all the whipped cream and nuts on them. Then I get sick from the motion on the ferry. You'd think I'd learn, but I just can't resist." The laugh that followed was weak and watery, but it was there.

Matt felt his deep respect for this woman grow. She was keeping the operation going in spite of whatever had crashed down on her today. What had they asked of her? What terrible thing had they demanded? Matt felt a murderous rage at those who would manipulate and control in such a way as to devastate a young woman. Then he checked himself. There was too much emotion here. He was getting too personal. He forced back the rage and emotionally stepped away. He had to maintain objectivity and a professional detachment. Lives depended on it.

"I'm sorry I scared you, Matt," Marta's voice pulled him back from his internal struggle. "I'm all right now. I think I'll go home and lie down awhile. Then I'll be just fine." She silently handed an envelope to Jane.

After Marta left, Jane opened the envelope and handed it to Matt with raised eyebrows. Matt silently counted out $5,000 in cash. He handed it to Jane to verify the count. They would drop this money off and pick up a packet to replace it. The serial numbers would be traced to see if they could determine how the money was laundered.

Rusty and Matt left Jane to monitor the surveillance equipment and went for a run so they could place the money in the drop box. When they were safely under the cover of the heavy traffic of Silverdale Way, Rusty began briefing Matt.

"She's to entice a senator's aide into a compromising situation. We checked out her target. He's a heavy-hitting staffer in Washington, and his dad is Air Force Major General Parsons. He's Senator Van Boren's top aide. The Senator's been good to us law enforcement types, is totally committed to our military actions over seas, and is death on the drug trade. That combination would make this Parsons kid an attractive target to any number of bad guys. Someone controlling him could get access to clandestine operations and through him could influence the type of information flowing to the Senator. The General could be compromised through his son in a number of nasty ways. The military and the CIA are uncomfortable as are we all.

We're not sure what we've stumble into here, Matt. If it was a straight foreign intelligence connection, it would be more predictable – unless Gorgonov himself is running it. That old fox is never predictable. He really is the creative master spy. Petrov Illianyich, the contact today, is more predictable, but he isn't the lead on this op. The CIA has quite a bit on this guy. He's evidently the expendable patsy – not a very nice expendable patsy, mind you. He's been connected with a couple of assassination attempts and some really nasty controlling behavior with some of the unfortunates he's recruited into his stable of informants. Some have come to us just to try and get some protection from him. His connections are hazy at best because he'll work for anybody who has money.

Matt, one of his KGB cover identities was Peter Alexander. It makes me sick that the KGB let him play 'daddy' to a little girl." Matt nodded in mute agreement. "Her assignment obviously didn't agree with her. That creep really put it to her, Matt. I've never wanted to punch somebody out so bad. It's rough to maintain professional detachment on this one."

Matt recognized Rusty's attempt to open the subject of his rather obvious problem with Marta. After all, it was not part of FBI surveillance procedures to take the target in your arms and let her sob on your shoulder. It was, however, part of his cover. He'd fall back on that excuse, which Rusty wouldn't buy.

"A part of my cover is showing more than a passing interest in the lady, but you obviously picked up on my intense reaction. She was just so sick. When I saw her coming up the stairs, I wanted to kill somebody. I've never felt such rage, Rusty. I need some prayer support on this one. I haven't even seen this guy Petrov and I already hate him. Forgiveness for what I saw today is going to come hard."

"Hate the sin, not the sinner," Rusty grinned. "Easier said than done, ain't it? We're all capable of the lowest depravity but for the grace of our Lord. And Jesus died for Petrov, too. Don't I just sound too pious? I want to destroy him as much as you do. He's desecrated the role of father and that hits me where I live. I keep thinking of my little Sally and how vulnerable she is. Then I think of Marta as a little girl with that monster as a dad. I guess Nicolai Androvich Gorgonov can't be all that bad if he protected her the way Marta said he did. I can't help but wonder why."

That caught Matt's attention. That was indeed an intriguing thought. Why would a ruthless master spy take the trouble to protect a young girl from one of his own network operatives? And what about the KGB mother, Tanya? How did she fit in? Obviously, she'd provided a lot of protection before Gorgonov showed up, probably at the risk of her own life. Then again, Gorgonov may have been involved all along without Marta knowing it until she was a preteen.

Rusty continued with his briefing, "She's to start hanging around the Silverdale Tavern. It's right here in the neighborhood on the main drag. There's an opening for a bartender, which we secured for you. It's just beer and wine, so no fancy training required. You start tonight at 7:00. The shrinking job market helps to explain why a devout Christian might take a job in a tavern."

"It sounds like everything is moving along. I take it I don't have to play the attentive Romeo now?" he asked hopefully. Taking Marta in his arms had been a grave error in judgment.

"Play it by ear. I understand it could get a little dicey for you to play such a part and remain detached. But, hey, you're FBI. You can do anything, right?" Rusty punched him on the arm to punctuate his little joke. "We may need that kind of scenario at some point, especially if we need to run interference or step in at some point without blowing our cover. After all, you may get to play the jealous boyfriend and punch out a senator's aide. Wouldn't that be fun?"

"You bet. I'm a professional FBI agent and punching out a senator's aide would be hilarious fun," Matt grinned at Rusty. They returned from their run, and Jane informed them that Marta was still asleep next door.

Across the way, Nicolai reentered his apartment and gave Tanya a questioning look. "She's still sleeping, Nicolai. I think she'll be all right. Did the FBI fill our opening at the tavern with one of their own?"

"Of course. It was too good an opportunity to miss. I just hope they don't see it as too opportune. The opening was legitimate. After all, I'm evidently supposed to think the network bought the disinformation that I returned to Moscow. I couldn't very well show up in my own tavern as a bartender tonight. Although, after today, I don't know what difference it makes. Someone knows who I am and that I activated Marta. They evidently don't know that Marta activated the FBI unless they are trying to get Petrov killed. A noble ambition, but why ruin my day while they do it?"

They laughed a rather forced laugh together, though each was far from secure in the triple jeopardy mission they found themselves running. They had to fool whoever was interfering with them, the FBI, and the maverick network of agents working for the highest bidder. The money trail led deep into the mountains on the border of Afghanistan and Pakistan, with branches off to Mexican drug cartels. Any of these could turn on them and bring certain death…or worse.

They were uncertain what the FBI would do with them, but if things turned liquid the FBI was their best bet for protection… for themselves and for Marta. Deportation would not be a bad way to end his time in America, even if Marta had to face it as well. His network was busily humming along in every nook and cranny of the former Soviet Union, as well as internationally. Nicky's heart swelled with pride as he thought of the other patriots who had caught his vision. These were the builders of freedom, trained in the very best America had to offer, doing legitimate business, and standing courageously against the crime lords. For himself, though, he'd rather farm and leave the rest to the youngsters.

The sound of water running in Marta's shower brought him back to the present dangerous circumstances.

CHAPTER SEVEN

Marta stepped into the steaming shower and tried to get clean. The shower door was locked, a habit from childhood she suddenly reverted to after her brush with Peter. For a few blessed moments, her numbed brain thought about absolutely nothing but warm needles of water hitting her tense muscles. Reality soon returned. She thought of her target, Timothy Parsons, and what on earth she was going to do about him. Marta's whole strategy with men had been to keep them away. She had not the slightest idea what to do to attract one and she knew no one to ask. Wait! Jane might know, but how could she ask her without all the surveillance picking it up? If she did it under cover, it could be made to appear that she was trying to attract Matt, but that could get complicated.

She couldn't understand why Peter thought this was going to be such a cake walk for her. She had no idea what he meant by her assets, but the way he said it, they couldn't be very nice assets. Had they taught her something that marked her as cheap or easy? Is that why men always seemed to stare at her wherever she went? Marta felt the bile rising in her throat. She was suddenly sure they'd somehow marked her as ruined or dirty.

Hearing the doorbell, Marta reluctantly jumped out of the shower, grabbed her robe, and went to the door. Jane stood on the other side with a thermos. She crossed the threshold, closed the door and without a word, held open her arms. Marta felt that comforting, protective presence descend again upon her as she stepped into Jane's hug. Two people in one day had held her in their arms. She couldn't remember the last time anyone had hugged her.

"I brought chicken soup. What can I say?" Jane laughed as she released Marta and put the thermos on the kitchen counter, holding an envelope up for Marta's notice. So, the chicken soup was a cover to return the envelope. That was okay, but Marta wished again that a warm touch didn't always have to come as a cover for clandestine activity. Would she ever be free to have real friends?

Jane's joking manner broke into Marta's dark thoughts, "I'm just an old wife with lots of tales." Marta had to laugh at the mischievous expression on Jane's face. "Ah, now, that's music to my ears. You need to laugh more often, Young Lady, and I mean to set myself to see that it happens. Now, to the news. Matt has a job! We're glad for the salary; we need it. We're not so excited about the surroundings, but as taverns go, it's not all that bad." Jane winked at Marta's surprised expression.

"Yup, Matt's gone to work at that tavern on the main drag. He'll be making decent money plus tips, and the manager is actually glad he doesn't drink. So, are you feeling well enough to go over there and give him a little moral, no pun intended, support? We could have dinner. I understand they serve some pretty good food at that tavern. Rusty can eat his own burned pea soup. Ugh, can you smell it?" Marta just nodded. "Matt tried to choke some down before he left for work at seven. Do you think you'll be feeling well enough to eat by then? Say something so I'll know you're all right," Jane laughed.

"Yes, eight is fine," Marta tried to keep the quaver from her voice. "I'm really better, and I'll drink a little chicken soup just to fortify myself."

Marta held up her hand to keep Jane a minute while she scribbled a note. To cover the silence, Jane began chattering about what she was going to wear to dinner. Marta passed her note to Jane, and then took up the wardrobe chatter while she read it.

She watched Jane swallow as if she were having difficulty, then she wrote a response, handed it to Marta and took up the chatter.

Marta had asked what "assets" she could possibly have to attract some stranger. Jane had responded, "You're gorgeous! You'll do fine."

Marta was burning the note as Jane left the apartment with a cheerful "See you later," as she pantomimed flushing the toilet so Marta would be sure to flush the ashes. The humor of it hit them both at the same time, and their giggles covered the leave taking. Marta took care of the flushing ritual as soon as Jane was out the door. She then partook of her very first taste of homemade-with-love chicken soup.

Matt, on the other hand, was learning the intricacies of beer from the tap and bar snacks, interaction with the busy kitchen, finding replenishment stocks, and just how heavy a case of bottled beer can be. He was also keeping his eyes and ears open. The bureau hadn't yet been able to get him a photo and complete "bio" on Timothy Parsons. He only had Rusty's sketchy briefing to go on. Nor had they run down a complete ownership history on this bar. It would be extremely interesting to get all that information and see if it was the exact key they needed to break his previous case. He remembered standing with Frank in his office the day Marta had walked in, praying for a break. Incredible. How many times could such miracles happen before he'd start really expecting God to answer prayers just as He promised? He then left it all in God's hands as customers started to filter in, needing his attention.

In spite of all the wardrobe discussions, Marta wore a pair of jeans and a work shirt because that was all her wardrobe afforded. She had one dress, bought at the Good Will, her store of choice and budget. That dress was wrinkled and she had no time to iron it. She hoped that whatever Jane meant by gorgeous worked in jeans.

She went through the envelope Jane had brought with the Chicken soup and found it stuffed with ample money to enhance her wardrobe. She'd ask Jane to help her with some tips on "fixing up" as Peter had so crudely put it. She also found a photo of Timothy Parsons. The only information was his name on the back, but that made sense. She wasn't supposed to know anything about him, so that was one thing she wouldn't have to lie about.

A sharp rap on her front door brought Marta out of her reverie. It was Jane, so she pulled the door shut behind her. Jane called out to Rusty as they walked by the apartment next door, "We're leaving now, Honey. Sure you don't want to come?"

"I'm sure. I enjoy my split pea soup even if no one else does." Marta could hear the laughter in his voice as he leaned out the door and gave Jane a peck on the cheek. The two ladies then started walking briskly toward the Silverdale Tavern.

"Any butterflies about tonight?" Jane asked softly as they got to the more heavily traveled main street where traffic noise could better cover their conversation.

Having received the signal she could talk, Marta took her main chance, "I have no idea what to do when we get to this place, Jane."

"Just look for your man and take whatever opportunity comes. Don't worry; you'll do fine. If I see a chance to get the two of you together, I'll help. Don't count on me, though. Go after the guy."

"How?" Marta whispered.

"Well," she said slowly, "if he looks at you, smile or lift up a glass in a toast. Really I don't think you'll have any trouble at all. You've really never been out like this before?"

"Never!" Marta took a deep breath. "I've always avoided social contact. My life was just too complicated."

Jane nodded as if confirming something to herself. They went the rest of the way silently. The parking lot was only half full when they got there. They had no trouble getting a table as most of the patrons were in the game room. Most of the patrons were also male and, as if on some primal signal, they all turned and watched Marta and Jane as they made their way to an empty table. Matt turned the bar over to a waitress as they came in.

"Hey, Sis. Hi, neighbor," Matt came to their table from behind the bar. "What can I get you to eat and drink?" They ordered burgers and designer water. Matt hustled their food order to the kitchen and then released the waitress to work tables the rest of the evening. Jane set the tone of small talk signaling Marta to try and look like they were enjoying themselves. Marta decided to use the time to good advantage.

"Jane, I'm wondering if you could help me shop for some clothes. I got a big birthday check from an uncle and I thought I'd get some clothes with it. Maybe I'll get my hair done and stuff, too. I'd really like some advice."

"Are you kidding? I love to shop. It's my life, even if I can't spend anything on me. It's twice as much fun to spend someone else's money." From that point on they had no problem talking naturally.

They were so deep in planning their shopping spree, they almost missed the target when he came in. Jane did notice and nudged Marta, signaling with her eyes as the young man came in with a large group of jostling jocks, dressed in running shorts and tee shirts from various runs across the nation and around the world. All were obviously affluent, successful, and accustomed to drawing the attention of the female population. Marta had dealt with their kind before, and her heart dropped to her toes. How could she hope to attract one who had the adoration of beautiful women wherever he went? She'd seen how women vied for attention from such men.

By this time there were a number of couples and a few single women in the tavern. Some of the single women were at the bar, making Matt's life somewhat difficult, though he was handling it with charm. Marta felt a twinge of something, a rather startling and unpleasant emotion, as one of the women openly flirted with

Matt and he responded with gentlemanly grace. She didn't have time to deal with feelings right now, so she shut them off.

There were still, however, mostly single men in the bar, added to by the group who'd just come in. Some were openly staring at Marta and, as evidenced by some of the jostling and joking, a couple of them were trying to get up the nerve to come over. Not so Marta's target. He had the cool confidence of the sought after. He looked in her direction only twice, once to order his beer and once to pay for it. Neither time did he make eye contact with Marta; neither time did he show any sign that he even noticed her. It was going to be a long night.

The wolves around the bar began to advance upon Marta and Jane. Jane, protected by the obvious wedding ring on her left hand abandoned Marta to their concentrated efforts. Jane's eye danced. Marta could have kicked her as guy after guy came over wondering if he could buy her a drink or interest her in a game of darts or…anything.

After the fifth one, Jane had evidently had enough, "Oh, please, Marta, play darts with the poor kid so I can eat my burger in peace." Marta gave her a withering glance, but obliged, seeing that the dart game would put her into the target's line of vision. Jane was good. She'd spotted an opportunity and pushed her to take it in the most natural way imaginable.

He looked at her not once during ten miserable games of darts in which Marta actually hit the board a few times. Of course, all the guys in the game room, the concentration of which had markedly increased since Marta's advent there, thought her lack of skill quite charming. They loved it, each one vying for more of her attention than the next. Marta caught Matt's eye. He was obviously amused. He would pay.

The only guy who seemed to be paying her no attention at all was the one she was supposed to be targeting. His friends had even begun watching her dilemma in somewhat superior amusement. He, however, had retreated behind, of all things, a book!

He was reading intensely as if catching up on some work while his friends were otherwise entertained – at her expense!

Marta felt, for the first time in her life, feminine offense. Her eyes narrowed as she concocted a bold plan. "All right, you guys, no more darts! I have a very cold burger waiting for me, and I'm going to eat it, soggy bun and all."

"Let me buy you another."

"Bartender, the lady's burger is cold. Bring a hot one."

"Come on, Babe. I'll take you for a steak."

The cacophony of offers played right into her plan. She couldn't believe she was actually going to do this. Her stomach fluttered and she took a deep breath. She pretended to lose her temper. "Hold it! Just a minute! I'll eat my own cold burger and that's that. The only guy in this bar that's left me in peace all night is reading a book over in the corner, and I'm going to buy him a beer in appreciation. Bartender, a beer for the gentleman with the book," she gestured grandly toward Timothy Parsons. "Put it on my tab."

She held her head high, playing the part of the offended princess to perfection, while inside a terrified little girl wondered how she was going to hold down the burger she now had to eat at all costs. Years of training and discipline came to her aid. She was a professional, every inch of her. She blessed Tanya in her heart for making her tough enough for this night.

She made it back to the table, reading admiration in Jane's eyes. She bit into her hamburger as if ravenous. The bar was deadly quiet for a moment of two. Then deep male guffaws came from behind the book. Humor exploded around them as Marta and Jane joined in with the laughter. Marta noticed that Matt had to hold his side and wipe a tear from his face as he delivered the beer with the panache of the court jester.

After that, everyone was friendly but gave her space. Marta was accepted as a regular, and, best of all, Timothy Parsons was on his way over to her table.

"I hope you won't take the beer back if I join you?"

"Of course not. I didn't mean to disturb or embarrass you, but it was getting a bit much with those guys."

"Hey, most of them are submariners. You stick a guy in a steel tube for six months with a bunch of other guys and he gets a little bit crazy the next time he sees a woman, especially one as lovely as you."

Marta blushed, unsure of what to say. It didn't matter because Timothy was an excellent conversationalist and soon found a subject they held in common – running. She hardly noticed when Jane left the table to join Matt at the bar. By the end of the evening, Timothy knew about everything she could tell him about herself. She also knew a great deal about him, including that he worked for a senator on a powerful committee. She was disturbed to find that Timothy was a charming man. She didn't exactly like him, but his charisma was a bit hypnotic. It was going to be hard to use him and possibly put him in danger. She hoped the FBI would brief him and give him a choice about cooperating or backing out. But that was not her concern. She had to do her part the best way she knew how, and she would.

Matt's voice giving last call for alcohol broke into the quiet conversation between Marta and Timothy. They looked up to see the tavern almost empty.

Matt's grin appeared somewhat strained as he called out to them, "You two want anything more from the bar? This is your last chance."

"No, no thanks," Timothy smiled after a questioning look at Marta. They'd gone through numerous bottles of water in the evening after Timothy had switched from beer to water after finishing the beer she'd bought him. "We're just a couple of runners whose favorite drink seems to be water." He gestured to a couple of empty designer water bottles still left in front of them. Matt nodded crisply and the waitress hurried to clean off their table.

"May I take you home, Marta?" Timothy asked her. Marta was unsure of what to say. Never having dated, she didn't know if it would look odd if she didn't let him take her home. Neither did she want to give signals that he could take liberties with her. She decided to play it safe.

"No, thanks, I came with my neighbor, Jane. She's the bartender's sister. They're neighbors of mine," Marta fumbled around.

He seemed to understand, "I'd like to see you again, Marta. Unfortunately, I'll only be here a couple of weeks. I actually am here a day earlier than I expected to be, but the price is that I do have some business to take care of in Seattle tomorrow. Could I take you to dinner tomorrow night?"

"I'd like that, but I have to work late tomorrow night. With the sun staying up so late in the summer, I'll be out until after 10. My realtors all want their pictures before the weekend. Could we make it the next night? I'll have a freer schedule then."

"Sure, great," he actually looked relieved. Marta was surprised. He seemed so self-assured; she thought he would surely assume she wanted his company. It did not seem that he was all that sure of her. Perhaps that was good. She gave him her phone number. She didn't give her address yet, unsure of how the FBI wanted her to handle him and not wanting to put either of them at any more risk than absolutely necessary.

The light went out over the bar. Matt was out helping the waitresses wipe off tables. Jane came over to their table, pulling a light jacket over her shoulders.

"I know, a jacket in July," she laughed, "but coming to Washington from California means we are freezing in what you people have the audacity to call summer!"

Timothy gave his deep rumbling laugh again and looked with chagrin at his running shorts and tee shirt. "Although I'm a native, I'm glad I brought a car to keep warm in. The other Washington was a sweat box when I left this morning, and I'm not used to much cool weather either. I'd be glad to run you ladies home in my car, but Marta tells me you've come together and are all set to go home together. My sports car has no back seat, so I could only take one of you."

"We're fine," Jane responded firmly, confirming Marta's decision. "Matt's going to see us home safely, but thank you for your consideration."

"Well, then, if you ladies don't need my macho protection any more this evening, it's been a very long day. It's about five a.m. in the other Washington now, and I'm beat."

His friends were gathering at the door, obviously impatient for him to leave. He acknowledged them and got up, shaking hands first with Jane, then turning to Marta, "Until Thursday evening then?" She nodded as she shook his hand. He waved to Matt as he left with his friends. Matt made a gesture back that didn't look awfully friendly to Marta but could have been taken as a wave. Jane raised here eyebrows at Matt, but nothing was said as he finished his last chores.

It felt good to walk out into the cool July night with Jane and Matt. She had enjoyed Timothy's company; he'd been very entertaining, but there was definitely something missing with him that wasn't missing with Matt. Marta had no idea what. She was only glad that Matt was taking her home, not Timothy. Silly girl. He was only doing his job.

The effects of the long day and evening began to tell on her. She had shut off all feeling for far too long. She was going to pay a price for that, and the bill started coming due about a block away from their apartment building. Her knees grew weak. The nausea of earlier in the day returned. Her muscles clenched then went weak again. Dizziness began to plague her as the world began to spin slowly, then more quickly. Jane took her arm in alarm. Then Matt's arm was around her, practically holding her up.

"Just another block," he whispered gently next to her ear. His breath against her ear added other, disturbing, inexplicable feelings to her already unbearably complex emotions. She felt the bile rise, her legs buckle.

"Boy, you really can't hold much, can you, Kid?" Jane joked loudly enough to cover Marta's obvious distress and inability to navigate on her own. "I guess that burger on an already sick stomach didn't go over too well, huh? Think you need a doc?"

Alarm sounded in Jane's tone. Marta shook her head weakly to indicate an adamant negative on the doctor. The movement caused the world to spin around her. Matt suddenly picked her up and headed for the apartment as fast as her weight would let him move. Jane grabbed her purse and got out her keys to get her inside as quickly as possible.

"I'll get the 7-UP and crackers, Matt," Jane said after letting them into Marta's apartment.

Marta again found herself in a bathroom with Matt holding her head. He gently held her, wiping her face with a damp wash cloth left from her earlier shower. He carried her to her bed and lay down with her, holding her. Great, silent sobs shook her body, and still he held her, stroking her back. Tears were soaking his shoulder. She could feel the spreading moisture as it soaked his shirt. She was so humiliated, yet she couldn't stop. All the pent up longing and loneliness of all the cold, empty years poured out, and she wanted Matt to hold her forever. He made her feel safe. Timothy didn't. Under all his charm, she knew without a doubt that he cared nothing for her except for some inexplicable demand she felt from almost all men, a demand that left her feeling threatened, alone, in danger, bereft of care. Only with Uncle Nicky and now with Matt had she ever felt safe in the presence of a man. In that safety, leaving behind all the perplexity of new experiences and feelings, the blessed healing oblivion of sleep came to Marta.

Matt held her until he was absolutely sure she was asleep. Jane returned and stopped dead in the doorway, Mat could see from the dim light through the Venetian blinds the shock on her face.

"Shh," he whispered, "she's asleep. Poor kid. That burger must have been a real gut bomb after being sick this afternoon."

Jane's face relaxed from shock to understanding. Matt was disturbed that she could think what she had obviously been thinking, but then, who wouldn't? There they were on her bed. Trying not to wake her, he gently moved away. She didn't flicker an eyelash, obviously exhausted beyond all endurance. No wonder. She'd been through an emotional meat grinder at least twice today. He moved his right arm carefully from under her. She groaned and wriggled to a more comfortable position, for her, not for Matt. She didn't awaken, so he got the rest of the way up. She rolled into the space he left open and continued to slumber. So much for being missed. He gave a wry look at Jane, but it was too dark for her to see. Just as well.

They tiptoed out of her bedroom, closing the door behind them. Jane put the soda and crackers on the counter where Marta would see them if she needed them in the night. They vacated the apartment as quietly as possible and entered next door where Rusty was catching a nap on the couch so he could take up the vigil when they got home.

Matt shook him gently and he came alert, silently. He nodded and vacated the couch. Matt sank into the warm place Rusty left, watching him make a cup of instant coffee from the hot water pot they kept filled. His last conscious memory was the feel of Marta in his arms. It was good, too good.

CHAPTER EIGHT

Matt's arms were around her. Marta felt so safe, so warm, slipping further and deeper into his embrace. Peace and safety. But no, the arms changed, becoming hard. Hands grabbed at her and she found herself running for her life, but she could go no faster. They were gaining on her. She could hear them breathing. Fingers like claws tore at her flesh. She turned to fight. Peter! No! The hate in his eyes, his loathsome leer, he had her. She was in his power. He was dragging into darkness, horror. She tried to cry out, but no sound would come. She was helpless, helpless. There was no power in her. What had Rusty said that morning? About God? It was okay with God if she had no power. He had all the power needed to save and protect her. She knew that was right. She prayed to Matt and Rusty and Jane's God. She cried out in her helpless terror and the tearing talons let her go.

She sat straight up in the darkness of her own bedroom. A dream, it had been a dream, yet its effects stayed with her. She was in very real danger, but the sense of protection and caring was also very real and very present. She lay back down, thinking about the strange breakfast she had shared with three FBI agents. Had that been this morning or yesterday? She looked at her alarm clock, lighting up her bedside table with its weird green figures. Yes, it had been yesterday morning, for her clock told that, in spite of her exhaustion; she was waking up at her usually pre-dawn running time.

She would be expected to sleep in this morning, and she needed time to think, if not to rest. She lay very still to ensure the listening and watching world would get no hint of her awakening. She struggled with what they had said at breakfast yesterday about God and Christ. It didn't match her view of ultimate power. If she had a view it was of someone just plain mean. If someone was really in control, that someone had left her alone and helpless since earliest infancy in the hands of some of the most horrible people in the world. That someone had allowed her to be put in the untenable position of being raised by people who didn't love her, who just wanted to use her to gain power for themselves. Now, she was entrapped in a scenario with people showing her pretended kindness, offering acted love. Why? Their goal was to draw out of hiding not only the people she viewed as bad guys, but also her Uncle Nicky, the only person who had ever shown her kindness and affection. These same people were trying to convince her that an all-powerful being was Love? Fat chance.

Anger boiled up in Marta. Its intensity overwhelmed her. In a silent scream, she challenged that ultimate power. "How can you say you love me when you've let all these bad things happen to me? I was just a baby. You should have protected me from bad people!"

Tears fell, and the deep silent sobs of anguish came from a well of sorrow Marta herself had never touched or acknowledged. It was too late. The silent scream had been unleashed, and the anguish of unbearable loneliness engulfed her. She was drowning in it.

A sudden, unspoken command to stop came from within herself but also from beyond herself. The universe seemed to stand still, waiting in breathless silence for something momentous to happen. Marta knew she was about to get some sort of answer to the questions she had so thoughtlessly thrown at a Power great enough to create a universe. She suddenly knew, beyond a shadow of a doubt, that not only did that power exist, but that He was here and He was about to answer her charges.

She would have died in terror had not Rusty's morning prayer come back to her in snatches: "Heavenly Father...abundant care...precious Son...redeeming sacrifice for our sin...give us Yourself in our hearts and lives. Your presence...treasure beyond price. Your care...." She knew that the One Rusty had prayed to was here with her. She couldn't see Him. There were no visual or sound effects, no heralding trumpets or winged creatures. But He was here with her. He was asking entry. He was requesting her permission to...what? Why should such a One need to ask? He could just take what he wanted, couldn't He? She had no idea what to do. Then she remembered her silent prayer for help yesterday afternoon. Shame engulfed her. She'd just yelled accusations at the One from whom she'd asked help.

Somewhere she'd heard, perhaps from a bothersome stranger on the street one day, "All have sinned and fallen short of the glory of God." The words had been nonsense to her then but not now. Now it made sense. She'd never understood what people meant by sin, not crime, but sin.

She concentrated on the phrase "the glory of God." *The glory of God, the glory of God,* echoed through her as she began to sense, catch a tantalizing whiff, of what the glory of God meant. The quivering, sublime ecstasy of a glory fulfilled, not only fully meeting all expectations, but all hopes and dreams, all imagination of what glory might mean, but so far beyond it that...that...what? To experience it would be your undoing, but it was worth being undone to experience it. "All have sinned and fallen short of the glory of God." To have a taste, yet know she couldn't possibly be welcomed into that experience was the deepest misery. She had accused and challenged. Yet, He was here. He was asking. What had Rusty said about His Son? She'd heard so much about Jesus Christ and paid absolutely no attention. How could she have been so stupid?

She had been rude to that annoying presence on the street, that person who had bolstered enough courage to talk to her, but the words came back now in her moment of greatest need. She blessed that unknown person in her heart. "While we were yet sinners, Christ died for us." The impact of those words hit Marta at her very core. She didn't know how; she didn't know why, but those words meant she could be welcomed into that glory which waited. She thought of Christmas. Giving. The giving of gifts. Was she to give Him something? Wait, Rusty had said so much in his prayer about the Heavenly Father giving things… food, shelter, family… and His Son as a redeeming sacrifice so He could even give us Himself! She was to be the recipient of a gift…a gift so great it left her breathless. The universe waited for her to receive His gift, to receive Him. This presence that waited was for her, not against her. He wanted her to open up to Him somehow and let Him in. Because of Christ, she was to be treated as a friend, not an enemy. She could come to Him with nothing to offer but her aching need for Him.

A little voice within her asked, "Is that true?"

The fullness of Glory answered that it was indeed true. Marta reached out in a physical gesture, hardly knowing what she did. Her whole being said yes to this One who waited. In that moment, Marta Alexander abandoned herself to Love.

Matt listened intently, thinking he heard a small cry from Marta's apartment. There was no other sound, not even the sound of the deep, even breathing of sleep. It was, in fact, too silent. Matt strained to hear. Surely she was breathing, just softly. He was sure he'd heard a cry. Was it a cry of distress or a bad dream? Then why was it so silent? Why wasn't it followed by the sounds of rolling over and going back to sleep?

These were highly charged circumstances. He was tired. He was over-reacting to the pathos of this woman-child with wide blue eyes, raven hair, and the smoothest, creamiest skin. Whoa! He was attracted to her. That was no secret. He could absolutely not let that interfere. He was a Christian. This was just another temptation. There was a way of escape; he just had to find it. But the silence over there called to him.

Finally, he could stand it no longer. He had to make sure she was safe. There were too many others, friendly and hostile, who were listening to that unnatural silence, too. He could almost feel the palpable tensions from all those listeners. He looked at the clock. He saw the gray beginnings of dawn sneaking through the blinds and knew he had his excuse to go over. It was time to run. He'd check on her to see if she was sleeping in or wanting to run. It would be perfectly natural, wouldn't it? He hoped so as he changed into running shorts and a tee shirt.

He knocked but got no answer. He waited. He prayed for wisdom, wishing now that they'd used the excuse of her sickness last night to leave Jane with her. He used his body as a shield to cover the use of the key Rusty had given him, and turned the knob, his other hand close to the small gun hidden under his wind breaker. Pushing the door open with his body to keep his hands free, he cautiously entered. He nudged the door closed behind him and checked out the small living and dining area, then made his way with excruciating care through the tiny kitchen to the bedroom door he himself had closed too few hours before.

He saw her kneeling by her bed on the floor in a posture of absolute surrender. He felt the first tingle of fear at the base of his spine. What had happened? Had she given up in the face of the terrible odds that faced her? Had the realization of the danger she'd put her beloved Uncle Nicky in been too much for her fragile emotions? Then she looked up. He saw the tears sparkling on her face. She stood with such grace, such dignity, his heart constricted within him. Her face shown in the light of dawn with such radiance he knew it could have come from only one source. It was the radiance every Christian longed to see on the face of loved ones and strangers, friends and enemies, rescuers and tormentors. She had met her Savior and had fallen to her knees before Him. This radiance on the face of another made it worthwhile to remain in the dark world where Satan passed to and fro seeking whom he could devour. The radiant presence of Christ in the blush of first love made it worth every resisted temptation, every physical, emotional, or spiritual torment inflicted by the enemy of all life.

Matt felt the grin start as all of heaven smiled with him. There was a celestial party of major proportions going on right now. He wished all the silent listeners could hear it. The angels were rejoicing. The Father was crying out that one who was lost had come home.

For some moments they simply stared at each other, smiling through tears. Matt forgot all else, forgot all the silent listeners monitoring each sound, each word. In the glory of the moment, he forgot all else but that His Savior had picked up a lost and wounded baby lamb and carried her to safety in His arms.

"You've met my Lord Jesus Christ." Matt broke the magic silence with a statement not a question.

"Yes." She said it softly, the awe in her voice humbling him, drawing him back to those first moments in his own walk with the Prince of Heaven.

Matt came to alert as he heard the front door open. Jane came in and looked from one to the other, silently questioning what was happening. She rose magnificently to the occasion to protect their cover.

"So, Little Brother, you thought to drag her out to run after she's been sick twice, *twice*." Her voice rose to a crescendo on the second "twice." "I thought we agreed last night to let her sleep. She's been sick, but, no, you runners are obsessed. I don't' know how many times he's told me," Jane turned her tirade on Marta, "that he could run off any sickness. Well, not this time," she enunciated through clenched teeth. "I draw the line at dragging a sick person out of bed at the crack of dawn to run five miles. What is wrong with you people? Girl, you get those running shoes off and crawl back into that bed this instant. You are on soda, crackers, and chicken soup this day, do you read me? And you, you big lump, march out of here this minute…you irresponsible…you…man, you."

"Me," Matt responded in highly defensive tones, as a brother would to a sister's tirade, "I just came to see if she was up, and what did I find, huh? What did I find, responsible sister dear? An unlocked front door which came right open when I knocked! Who was the last one out of here last night?"

Jane looked horrified for a moment, but Matt held up the key to assure her it was just part of the act, knowing he doomed himself to long explanations from all quarters later.

"Oh no!" Jane entered into the charade, giving Marta a warning look as she saw a giggle shaking her lightly clad shoulders. "Are you all right? Did anything happen?"

"Well," Mat said mysteriously, "Nothing bad happened. Marta will tell you all about it later. We'll just be really careful to lock doors from now on, won't we, hmm?"

Jane gave him a look that confirmed to him that he'd pay dearly later. "We'll be leaving now, both of us. We will secure your door quite properly, and you will get back into that bed and *go to sleep!*"

"Yes, Ma'am." Marta saluted, unable to hold back the laughter a moment longer, her giggles becoming quite audible. She collapsed on the bed.

Jane marched Matt back to their apartment and loudly regaled the sleepy Rusty with the insanity and obsession of runners. Rusty slowly raised an eyebrow as Matt silently gave him Marta's apartment key. Matt could almost read his thought, "most unprofessional behavior." He could imagine the lecture Frank would have for him later. It was worth it. Matt grinned. He couldn't help it. Marta was saved. She was a member of the family of God. Nothing else would ever be as important. He wondered if Rusty knew, if he'd been listening. There had been just two soft sentences, but they'd be on tape, enhanced, analyzed, taken apart, and put back together. Matt frowned. The most intimate moment in person's life, and she would not even have privacy in that.

Rusty gave him a searching look, but he shook his head and mouthed, "Later." Rusty nodded. Matt then went for a solitary run to confirm the act they'd played out in Marta's apartment. When he came back, he found the three of them in a group hug, tears in every eye. He threw back his head and laughed out loud.

"Yes!" Matt did a little victory dance, "We left the door open and the Good Shepherd came in and made Himself at home. Ain't life grand?" Matt grinned benevolently upon them all.

"Grand it may be, my friend, but you have some penance to do for trying to manipulate a run from this young lady," Jane announced in a voice that brooked no argument. "You have to help us shop today."

Matt's face fell in dismay. "No, no, not that, anything but that! There can be absolutely nothing worse than a shopping trip with two women. Rusty, surely you need my help today?" Matt cried out in exaggerated pleading.

"You're on your own, man. I'm not getting into this. No way." Rusty held up his hands as if warding off a blow. "I have a job in North Kitsap County today." This let Matt know the command post was at the Kitsap County office rather than the Seattle office. It made sense to not be at the mercy of ferry schedules, and it would look more natural to go from Silverdale to North Kitsap for construction jobs. There was a booming construction industry going on there. He would try to get there before he went to work at the Tavern tonight. Maybe he could steer the shopping trip in that direction. He caught Jane's eye and saw she was thinking the same thing.

After finishing the last few photos in the Silverdale area, Marta enjoyed letting Jane drive so she could just soak in the scenery on the way from Silverdale to Poulsbo. They decided to skip the obvious shopping places like the mall in Silverdale and took the scenic route into the small Scandinavian town of

Poulsbo. Matt was very quiet in the back seat. Marta understood that he was on duty, watching for a tail. They made no real effort to clear their path, she noted.

"Do you want to shop in downtown or in the newer shopping areas off the highway?" Jane asked.

"Oh, downtown, please," Marta replied. "For the first time in my life I have enough money in my pocket to go to a little boutique on the main street. I've gone in there often just to drool over their clothes, but their prices were beyond my budget."

"Sounds like a plan to me," Jane said with satisfaction.

They passed through an older shopping district in Poulsbo Junction, rife with auto sales lots, and wound around Liberty Bay into the quaint downtown area. It was like driving into a northern European village, complete with murals depicting mountain scenes and folks in Scandinavian costumes. Marta had recently run the Viking Fest Race into this little downtown and enjoyed the festival afterward. It was an exciting street fair with costumes, a lutefisk eating contest, Nordic dancing, a parade, a food fair, and even a street dance in the evening.

Jane finally found a parking space between Poulsbo's charming downtown shopping street and the waterfront with its marina and Liberty Bay Park, a ribbon of green between asphalt and water. They piled out like small children on a school field trip. The town was crowded enough with tourists to make it exciting without being wearying.

"Let's go straight to your shop, Marta," Jane suggested. "Then we can have lunch in that wonderful Italian place I've heard so much about."

"Italian?" Matt scoffed, "What happened to Scandinavian cuisine?"

Marta laughed, "I can't think of a place that serves it! I think they use up all the lutefisk during their Viking Fest. Sorry, too late."

"Whew. That's good to know. I'm not a raw fish guy, not even Sushi," Matt swiped his brow in exaggerated relief.

They entered Marta's favorite boutique, laughing at Matt's antics. Marta greeted the proprietress excitedly, "Today I intend to actually buy something!"

"Wonderful. You've broken my heart for years coming in here and looking as if you longed to take half my store home with you. What are you looking for today?" asked the elegant shop owner.

"Everything," Marta responded with glee. "I just received a birthday gift from an uncle and I have nothing in my closet that didn't come from Good Will – not that I'm knocking Good Will. I've found some super bargains there and I'm sure I'll go back when the birthday money runs out. I've got to make the best possible use of this money for a good foundation wardrobe. That's why I came here. You have lots of wonderful things that can be thrown in the washer and dryer. I can't afford to invest in dry-clean-only stuff."

"Are you looking for office, casual, day time, evening? How can I help you?"

Marta cast a quick glance at Jane as she answered, "Not office. I work for myself and can wear almost anything. I'm a photographer by trade, and my clients are used to my bohemian look. I suppose I should have some versatile stuff that could be for new client meetings and other things," Marta said thoughtfully. "The main thing for now is that I met a guy and he wants to take me out for dinner tomorrow night. Who knows what after that, so I'm looking for a…." Marta again looked toward Jane hoping for some suggestions, and then noticed Matt trying to look very small in the background. He wasn't succeeding.

"Romantic look for daytime and evening," Jane finished for her. "We've brought my brother here to give the token male input."

"Thanks a bunch, you two. We now know who buys lunch, Sis!" His glower took in both women. Marta could tell he was teasing, but there was a sense of tension under his remarks. She'd forgotten again. He was armed. He was alert to a duty she'd completely forgotten. Because he'd come with them, she and Jane could just enjoy being girls in an expensive boutique with several thousand dollars burning a hole in their pocket. She sent her gratitude to him with a look and a smile. He gave her a silly grin and a mock bow. The proprietress laughed at their teasing as she moved among her treasures and selected several items.

"Would you like to try these to start, or would you rather go through and chose for yourself?"

"Both!" Marta cried. "I'll try these and then I'll go through and pick some others. You guessed my size. How did you do that?"

"Practice, my dear, practice. I hope you don't mind, but I've been dressing you in my mind every time you came in here. I actually tried to work up the nerve to ask you to model for me when a group of us had a show last year, but I couldn't quite bring myself to do it."

"I'd love to model clothes for you sometime for the opportunity to do some photo work between times. I've never shot anything like that and would like to try my hand at it. If I have a flair for it, I might be able to expand my business for the smaller shop owners who can't afford Seattle prices for a fashion photographer." Marta hugged the selections given her and headed for the small dressing rooms at the back of the shop.

Matt was bedazzled as Marta appeared in color after color, style after style. She was a princess on a fairy tale ride, getting ready for a ball with her prince…and he wasn't the prince. At that moment, he came very close to hating Timothy Parsons. Matt continued to watch, fascinated as she came out in a long skirt with a dark burgundy top. The color on her was phenomenal. Her eyes became an iridescent shade of deep blue. Her face bloomed with rose and porcelain complementing the dark brows, high cheek bones, and full, luscious lips. Matt prayed for strength. He was, he explained quite carefully to God, only a man. He was a man who wanted this woman as deeply and passionately as a man could want. He wanted no one else ever to touch her or hold her. He wanted no one to ever hurt her. He wanted to be the protector who kept her from harm.

"Don't look so fierce, little brother. It's almost over." Jane dug an elbow in his ribs to bring him back to the present. Matt jumped, realizing he had not been protecting at all. He'd left Jane without backup, pursuing his own selfish thoughts. He covered as best he could.

"Yeah, right," he said gruffly. Stretching, he rotated his head to take in their surroundings. He'd asked that their chairs be placed so they could see both Marta and the door, teasing that he wanted his escape route in full view. He took in the street, looking for familiar faces. He realized that, for who knew how long, anyone could have been peering in at them and he wouldn't have noticed. He did notice that there were a few more customers in the shop. That was scary because they were all watching Marta. He couldn't blame them. She was a natural model and showed the clothes to perfection.

"You," the proprietress addressed Marta, "are definitely in next year's show. I've already sold two of the outfits you wore today and you're drawing a crowd."

He and Jane exchanged a glance that meant it was time to get out of there. Marta was coming out of the dressing with several items to add to the growing pile at the cash register. When had she chosen all that? She caught his glance and an unspoken message passed between them. He'd seen married couples do it a million times, signaling each other that it was time to leave. Matt had always thought it took years of marriage to develop that nonverbal communication, but here he was in complete synchronization with a woman he'd known less than a week.

"Okay," Marta said, "I hope I've made the right choices. You weren't much help, Matt. Jane, dragging him along may not have been the best of ideas."

"Oh yes it was. I knew exactly which outfits he liked. His eyes got really round and his neck bulged a bit to let me know he was resisting the urge to actually say something nice. You see, if he had, he knows he'd be stuck taking me shopping all the time to give opinions on clothing. The only way men get out of these shopping trips is by never saying anything but, "Oh, that's fine, dear." If we ever got real feed back, they know they'd be sentenced to this torture for life."

"Can we just get lunch now, please?" Matt asked in a pained voice to go along with the cover they were giving him.

Matt watched Marta pay; concerned at the wad of money she withdrew from her purse. He made a mental note to tell her to deposit any cash she had left and write checks. He noted she carefully kept the receipt to keep a full account of the money.

CHAPTER NINE

Matt carried Marta's purchases and they deposited them in the convenient parking lot before going to the Italian place for lunch. Matt was pleased with the hearty selections on the menu and ordered a man-sized lunch to sustain him through the rest of the shopping trip. He hoped, though, that he could skip more shopping by slipping away on the excuse of finding Rusty. He'd get a golden opportunity to check in at their command post in Kitsap County. Jane and Marta might be able to check in too if it wasn't too risky.

After lunch, Jane nixed Matt's plan by suggesting that Matt and Marta take a walk while she called Rusty on his cellular to get directions to the "construction site." Matt would play it by ear as to whether he or Jane would go in to the "construction site," code word for the Kitsap command center, or if all three of them would be going. Jane would get her instructions and signal him somehow. In the meantime, he intended to enjoy this time alone with Marta. He kept his inner antenna alert for danger but gave himself the luxury of enjoying walking next to a woman who could keep pace with him without getting breathless. They headed with one accord to the promenade at the end of Liberty Bay Park. A board walk wound along Liberty Bay with little benches built in here and there. Although the day was cloudy, there were sun breaks, and it wasn't raining…yet. The view across the water was spectacular. They stopped once or twice to take in the marina with its bobbing forest of masts, the sparkling water in shades of green and quicksilver, the multiple greens of the hillside dotted with houses and an old red barn bespeaking the area's agrarian past. The mountains played hide and seek with the clouds, giving glimpses of towering peaks in shades of blue, brown, and green with shining white snow fields still clinging to the highest crags.

Matt found his hand had somehow entwined itself with Marta's. They needed no words, just drank in the beauty of the peaceful scene before them as if storing it for retreat in more violent moments. They reached the end of the board walk and climbed a set of stairs onto a winding trail arched above by trees and surrounded by foliage. It was like stepping into another world of fairies and dancing ferns where the noise of the clumsy inventions of man did not fully penetrate the hushed mystery of the green world.

Still hand in hand, they reached a little aside where the trees arched over a majestic madrona tree growing straight out toward the water instead of up toward the sky. It was like a little grotto inviting them to enter. They leaned back on the madrona, letting it hold them up as they visually explored their little room. Marta touched Matt's arm in the quiet. He saw a troubled look marring the peace of this place. Suddenly he knew that the privacy afforded a rare opportunity to express her true feelings. She wrote a quick note on paper she pulled from her purse. The words burned themselves into his soul as he read them.

I don't want Timothy Parsons to be the first man to ever kiss me. It was a simple note. Her look spoke volumes more. She wanted someone who cared about her to give her that first kiss. She wanted him. He had won her trust. This note and her look said he had won her heart. Without further thought Matt answered her plea with purity and honor.

Her whole expression, body and soul, as reflected in her eyes, showed how fragile she was. He leaned slowly forward, his eyes locked on hers, his lips gently touching the soft velvet of hers. Echoing through his soul, Matt heard "What God has joined together, let no man put asunder." She was his and he was hers. Absorbing one another through their lips, they gradually entwined their bodies as a symbol of a more profound joining. Their souls touched in that moment, a moment they would remember for the rest of their lives.

Jane's voice calling him pulled Matt back to a present that enclosed both him and this woman he loved in ever-increasing danger. He lifted his head. Marta's eyes registered surprise, then question. Jane called again and Matt watched understanding replace the question in her eyes.

"We have to go back," Matt whispered softly. Marta gave a quick nod and turned toward the trail. It was almost physically painful to let her go. They had had their moment. He had been able to keep that one thing unsullied. How long before their circumstances would violate that moment? Unthinkable. Matt moved onto the trail with Marta just as Jane turned the corner.

"There you two are. I was worried." The tension in Jane's voice struck Matt full force. He'd done the unpardonable by disappearing in the middle of an operation with a key player. He should have stayed in the open, visible at all time, and close to the car. He'd have much to answer for when Jane got him back to the office. Matt gave her a sheepish look. It was apparent from her expression that she had a pretty good idea what had happened. He hoped she wouldn't assume it was something casual but would understand it was sacred and private.

"If you two are finished sightseeing," Jane continued, trying to maintain a teasing tone, "we have some shopping to do. This is serious business. I don't often get to watch that much money spent in one day. Speaking of that much money," she addressed Marta, "I'd feel more comfortable if you'd deposit your cash and use checks from now on. Seeing you flash that wad back in the boutique and then not being able to find you two gave me quite a turn. I thought you'd been robbed, murdered, and thrown into Liberty Bay." The reaming had begun. Jane was truly and profoundly angry. This did not bode well for Matt's career future.

Neither, however, did falling in love with an admitted sleeper spy. Oh, well. He'd been thinking about a career change anyway. His legal specialty was international law. He was fluent in Russian. So was his future wife. Whoa! Ground control was speaking again.

"So, let's go," Jane ushered them along. Matt realized he'd been standing there, staring stupidly at her, while his mind accepted a complete turn around in his life. Outside of church, the FBI had been his life. He'd just mentally given it up for one kiss. He forced his legs to move, following Marta and Jane out of fairy land and into reality. It had begun to rain. How appropriate. Jane kept up a light banter to which Marta was gradually able to respond. Matt came out of his dark reverie as they reached their car and Jane drove them to a shopping center on the highway heading to Bainbridge Island and the ferry to Seattle.

"Are you girls going to torture me this afternoon, too?" Matt asked, "Or have I done enough penance for trying to get Marta to run this morning?" The front seat exploded into laughter, breaking the pensive mood.

"I wondered when you'd start whining," Jane crowed. "Can't take it, huh? Well, even though you made not one actual comment this morning, I'll let you off. You can join Rusty at the construction site and be Macho Man the rest of the day. He'll bring you home with him. You'll need to remind him to leave the job in time to get you to work tonight."

"Yes, Mother."

"Shut up, you," Jane glowered at him in the rear view mirror. "Marta and I must get an evening gown before we rest. I'll drop you off at that supermarket. Rusty says it's just below the construction site, and you can walk the rest of the way to take him his lunch." Matt knew the place. There was an office building behind it in which the FBI sometimes rented office space. That must be the temporary command center for this operation. The supermarket was the perfect place to slip away.

After dropping Matt off, Jane headed to Silverdale and a formal boutique a little south of the mall. Marta wondered if even her wad would cover this. "Do you really think I'll need formal, Jane?" she asked shyly.

"Are you kidding? That guy you met last night is major league, Kiddo. Did you catch the running shoes? Custom stuff. I can't believe a runner wouldn't notice a thing like that."

Marta's dismay must have shown on her face. She usually did check out the running shoes of others at first opportunity. Her own shoes were the most expensive thing she owned, except for her camera. Jane chortled in triumph as the elegant proprietress approached. The woman quickly assessed their wishes and headed Marta to a dressing room where she began bringing selections. Marta stared into the mirror of the dressing room, a vision in sparkling pink. She had no idea how they did it but they'd gotten sparkling things all over a gauzy pink creation. It couldn't have been more suited to Marta if it had been created especially for her.

Jane whistled softly, "That's the very one."

"Okay, we'll set this one aside. Now," she said briskly, "let's try on everything else in the place, Jane. You can be my guide on how to wow a guy with custom running shoes. I've never met one before."

"What a quick study. I do believe you've mastered the art of mega-shopping in one afternoon." Jane grinned and the two began going through every rack.

Timothy did not like this one bit. He had walked into a senate staffer's worst nightmare when he had arrived home last night. An FBI agent waited there for him, looking extremely official. His first thought was to wonder who was under investigation, the senator or his mamma's only son? Either way it was bad and the timing couldn't be worse. The guy had said there was nothing to worry about. They just wanted his assistance on something and asked him to report to an office in Poulsbo the next morning. So here he was heading into some back street Kitsap County office instead of to his own office in Seattle where some very important work waited form him. The traffic was either getting much worse around here or he was in a very bad mood or both.

He finally found a parking space and went into the unobtrusive office building next to a construction site. Following directions to the unmarked suite, he located the guy who had come to his home. He entered a small conference room where another man in civvies and a couple of military types were waiting for him. This was worse than he thought. Surely there wasn't another mess like Iran/Contra going on. His stomach turned sour as he went over everything he knew, especially stuff going on right this minute in Mexico. Troops in Afghanistan had discovered some terrifying connections to Mexican drug cartels. While prying eyes were focused elsewhere, they were gathering as much intelligence and gaining as much footing as possible in Mexico to put those connections out of business.

The guy who seemed to be in charge stood and introduced himself as Frank, the FBI's Special Agent in Charge, and then went around the table introducing the others whose names flew right out of Timothy's fevered brain. Goodbye to his vacation plans. He wished the guy would cut to the chase so Timothy could begin damage control.

"How well do you know the young lady you shared a table with last night at the Silverdale Tavern?" one of the military types broke in with a heavy-handed interrogation style.

"The Snow Maiden?" Timothy was so shocked he forgot to fix the jerk with his intimidation glare and name off all the important contacts he had in the Pentagon who outranked this dude. The bartender from the Silverdale Tavern had come in just as he'd let the nickname male runner's had given Marta Alexander, a local runner who'd smoked way too many of them and was drop-dead gorgeous to add insult to injury.

"The Snow Maiden? That's what you call her?" the bartender challenged.

"You know her well enough to have a nickname for her?" the military type stated simultaneously and made a show of taking it down in his notes. Timothy decided it was time to take control of this little operation.

"Look, I say not one more word until I know what this is all about. Why am I getting the third-degree without benefit of a warrant or a subpoena? Who do you people think you are to demand my presence here?"

The man in charge, Frank, chose to answer that volley, much to Timothy's relief. "You have every right to know all that. The truth is we need your voluntary cooperation in something." Frank launched a warning look at the heavy-handed military guy and the antagonistic bartender. "I've prepared a full briefing for you. I think you'll want the Senator to be kept apprised as well."

This got Timothy's attention. If it involved his boss, he wanted the details and fast. "Go ahead, please," he acknowledged the FBI boss.

"The young lady you call the 'Snow Maiden' is named Marta Alexander. She came to us voluntarily to explain that she was a KGB sleeper spy who has just been activated by someone who knew her classified activation code. Are you familiar with the term 'sleeper spy'?" Timothy acknowledged that he was familiar with the term. That was about all that was familiar in this Twilight Zone. He could almost hear the theme song playing in the background.

"Are you telling me," he asked slowly and distinctly, "that the young lady who approached me last night is an admitted agent of the former KGB?"

"Yes. She was brought into this country as an infant and raised specifically to be activated on call by the KGB. We don't think they did this often. It wasn't a very effective program because there was no incentive but fear. That threat theoretically went away with the KGB and the Soviet Union. Even when the KGB was still active, the fear tactics seemed to drive the sleeper spies to come to us rather than work for the KGB. Their loyalty usually turned to America at some point. We had a number come in out of the cold, especially since the fall of the Soviet Union. We don't, however, know how many they sent. To tell the truth, I don't think they do either. We've asked and have been told that many of those files were stolen. Not a very comforting thought for either side."

"Interesting but how does this affect me and my boss?" Timothy asked.

"You're the target of some sort of operation. Ms. Alexander was just activated by someone using her defunct KGB code to gain some level of control over you. She's indicated she doesn't know why."

Timothy decided to do a little fishing to determine the level of knowledge in the room. "That's odd, though, isn't? I mean, the former KGB? What would they have to gain? Considering the committee my boss heads, I'd expect more trouble from domestic organized crime or from a more southward direction."

"There may be little difference or none at all. Frankly, Mr. Parsons, this operation does not follow what we've learned to expect from former KGB operatives who've gone rogue or from any other foreign intelligence agency, but then everything is in flux with global terrorism recruiting professionals from all available sources. We don't know what to expect from anyone any more. Matt here," Frank nodded to the bartender, "had the Russia desk for awhile back in DC and keeps his finger on the pulse. He tells me its like a sieve leaking elements of the old and the new merging and mingling as they flow outward. Some of this has been productive and we've been able to recruit some valuable resources ourselves, but most has been nightmarish." The bartender nodded affirmation. "Unfortunately, there may not be much difference between certain elements of the former KGB and international organized crime. The implications of targeting you and your boss are staggering."

Timothy went cold to the marrow of his bones. Staggering was an understatement. "Are you telling me that Mexican drug cartels may, in fact, be negotiating with elements of the former KGB, now aligned with organized crime, for weapons of mass destruction, possibly portions of a nuclear arsenal?" His words fell into a void of intense silence. He saw the possibility confirmed in the tension on the face of each person there. Timothy took a deep breath. That seemed to signal that it was time to breath again because everyone else followed suit.

"We do not know that," Frank stated firmly. "We have begun an authorized sting operation. We began that operation before we knew what Ms. Alexander's assignment would be. Upon being contacted, she simply came and offered herself to us. She has expressed a desire to be of whatever help she can. We are monitoring her every movement. So far, she has answered all tests of loyalty favorably. There is still some question. After all, it could the FBI, or any other element of the government," he gestured around the room, "who is the target. Ms. Alexander may or may not know the true target. It would not be the first time a beautiful woman has been painted as a victim requiring protection in order to gain trust, sympathy, information, etc." Timothy remembered hearing about some guy named Miller who'd traded secrets for sex. The Snow Maiden would be a prime candidate for that kind of operation, except she never let anyone near her.

The bartender evidently decided to get into the game. He'd been a bit bristly last night and Timothy had thought he was a contender for the beautiful Marta.

"You referred to Ms. Alexander earlier as the 'Snow Maiden.' Why?" The guy didn't waste words. Timothy had the uncomfortable feeling he'd had his mind read.

"You obviously didn't grow up around here," Timothy responded wryly. "Man, I knew it was too good to be true. I mean, right there, in front of all my running friends, the Snow Maiden put the moves on me. When she was a kid, this tall blond woman used to run with her in every race west of the mountains. My friends and I never saw them at any races except in the West Puget Sound area. Oh, they were in some Oregon races like the Rose Festival in Portland and the Sea Side Marathon a couple of times, but not every year like the local races.We called the blond the Arctic Queen because we assumed she was either her mother or coach and we naturally dubbed the younger girl the Snow Maiden. She and the Queen ran with a kind of arrogant grace that said, 'I could leave you in my dust but I choose not to.' They'd run just behind the contenders for third or fourth place, depending on how many would get a trophy or some recognition. It was like they just had to run as well as they possibly could without being noticed too much.

Every male runner my age in this area has tried to get near her. She was totally unapproachable. You couldn't even get her to make eye contact. It was like she had an emotional force field around her that repulsed anyone who tried to make contact.

A KGB agent, though, of all the theories, and we had a million of them, that never once occurred to any of us. Every guy runner in this area probably has a dozen fantasies about this lady." He noticed the bartender/agent bristle again. Definitely protective. He'd been bitten by the Snow Maiden bug too. "It was like she was Sleeping Beauty and we all wanted to be the prince who woke her up. Nobody even got close until last night. So, I was just an assignment. That hurts." Timothy shook his head in chagrin. There were a couple of females in the room, one in uniform, so he expounded no further. It was too humiliating. But from the look on every male face he knew they understood.

"Anyway," he continued, "the Queen disappeared years ago, triggering another flurry of attempts to reach her. The theory was that she was held back by her repressive mother or whoever. Still no luck, so everyone pretty much gave up. The local guys watched with amusement as the turnover of local sailors and marines took their shot. The races were about the only place to even try. One of my friends is a realtor and she takes pictures for him. He really thought he had the inside track, but she is strictly business.

I couldn't believe it when I saw her in a tavern last night. None of us could. I figured I'd already taken my best shots to get to know her and I had some hot research to finish for the Senator. When she bought me a beer, I thought I'd died and gone to heaven. You know, I didn't think of anything but her, getting close to her. Man, what a dangerous lady. I mean, I'm pretty paranoid because of my job, but I never even gave it a thought. I just dived in head first without a thought that she might be after me for information or to compromise me and gain control. This is a somewhat humbling experience on all fronts."

Timothy slumped a bit in his chair. He went over everything he could remember of what he'd said the night before and knew he'd compromised nothing. He hadn't even revealed his relationship to the Senator, or had he? Yes, he'd said something about his job. He knew that if things had progressed as he'd have liked them to, she probably could have pumped him pretty well. He shook his head in dismay, then asked, "I assume that, since you've told me all this, you have something you want me to do or was this just a warning visit?"

"Both," Frank answered, "we wanted to warn you and to ask you to continue the relationship." Timothy felt the tension in the room increase and knew they were ready to cut to the chase. The FBI spokesman continued, "We don't know exactly who these folks are and what their relationship is to the current Commonwealth. We're pretty sure what their relationship was to the former Soviet Union, though."

"Pretty sure?" Timothy asked.

"These folks appear to be tied to a network we've been working with the military to track down. This network was a KGB operation, a very successful one unfortunately. The methods it used disappeared for years after the Soviet Union fell, or at least didn't present themselves in a pattern we recognized. Then, a few years ago, we began noticing similar tactics and figured elements of the old network had either gone rogue or the intelligence agencies of the fragmented remnants of the former Soviet Union had reinstated those tactics.

We'd like your cooperation in a sting operation to uncover the current network, which appears to be a complete maverick. It matches the old network in methods but not operation. We've identified, from the young lady's descriptions, what appears to be a kingpin of the former KGB network, but we're unsure that this particular operation is sanctioned by any government.

Intelligence agencies tend to be fairly predictable, despite their best efforts. So far, this operation has been totally unpredictable."

"Sounds like it could be really dangerous." Timothy didn't want to look like a wimp, but this sounded like some serious stuff.

"I won't lie to you," Frank answered. "It is always dangerous to run sting operations. This one is especially dangerous because of what appears to be an alliance between international organized crime and a former intelligence network. You'd be right in the middle of it, but then you'd be right in the middle of it whether you worked with us or not. For some reason, you've become a target. It may be more dangerous not to work with us. It's your choice."

The agent's eyes never wavered from his. Timothy felt his stomach tighten and cold chills run up and down his spine as the import of those words hit him. He'd been in danger for some time and hadn't even known it. Suddenly a hunger to know who had targeted him became the over-riding emotion.

"I want to do this. Tell me how you want me to proceed." And thus, Timothy Parsons entered into a most dangerous game.

CHAPTER TEN

"Matt," Frank called to him as the meeting broke up and he was headed to the coffee pot. "They've set up a temporary office for us down here." He gestured toward the far end of the hall they were in. "I'd like a confab with you and Rusty."

Matt nodded and brought his cup of coffee as he followed Frank. Rusty quietly joined them as they entered an office with a view of the construction site next door. Matt knew from Frank's tone that the meeting did not bode well for him.

"What is going on with you, Matt?" Frank turned to him, concern written all over his face. "The military has specifically requested that I relieve you. They're not too awfully happy with the whole team although I backed them off in no uncertain terms on that score. They've objected strenuously to the evangelical activities. I reminded them that they had agreed to the cover for getting close very quickly to a reclusive personality. No Christian would have walked away from some of the opportunities Marta offered. They brought up that thing with you in St. Louis, Matt, where one of the drug dealers asked you a point blank question about Jesus and you kept your cover by telling him what you'd heard when you got dragged to Sunday school as a kid. That made you a two-strike in their opinion. The Bureau backed you on that one and we will on this one. Other behavior, however, such as entering the subject's apartment for some unknown reason and a rather strange conversation in her bedroom, is completely unacceptable. Add to that your disappearing act this afternoon with the subject and I've got a problem with you. What is this? Are you completely losing it?"

Matt could tell that Frank was mad. His unorthodox behavior was making it hard for Frank to protect the whole team. He shook his head, "Maybe I am losing it, Frank. I entered Marta's apartment simply because there was too much silence, a palpable silence coming over the surveillance equipment. I'd heard a small cry and then absolute stillness. I still can't explain it, but I felt we had some sort of crisis over there. I just went. I walked in, and she was on her knees by her bed. I entered no further than the doorway and didn't even notice she was still in her nightgown until Jane came in. She accepted Christ this morning, Frank. That's what the strange conversation was all about." Matt had to stop and swallow the lump in his throat before he could continue. "I wouldn't trade those few seconds for anything in life, Frank. If you could have seen the glory on her face…it was awesome."

Rusty broke in, "Frank, the military is going to have to accept that the Gospel is going to change lives, no matter the conditions under which it's preached. Our Christian faith may have presented a convenient cover for this particular operation, but the fact that it's a cover doesn't change its basic nature or our sincerity in living it out."

"I agree, Rusty, and I have no problem with that," Frank responded. "Matt, I want you to remember that we're in an extremely delicate situation here. You cannot give the appearance of evil. I'm not asking you to quench the Spirit. I will never ask that of you. Just remember, the world is going to hate you when you obey Christ. People have lost their jobs and worse. I may not be able to prevent such consequences…for all of us." His look took in Rusty, too.

Frank continued, "I'm willing to take whatever heat comes to stand with you if you are genuinely being led by the Spirit. Matt, you may have some other conflicts going on here, though. Your disappearance this afternoon was about the straw that broke the camel's back. I want the story on that."

"No excuse," Matt shook his head in contrition. "We stole a private moment. I don't even remember how we got out on that board walk. There was no decision. We just got there. She had a specific concern that she shared in writing and I responded to her concern."

"And the concern was?" Frank asked with both eyebrows raised.

"She…um…she's never been on a date before, Frank. She's grappling with things most girls deal with as teenagers." Matt felt the heat growing in his face. "She gave me a note that said she didn't want her first kiss to be from some stranger who didn't care about her." He wasn't able to look at Frank's face as he tried to relate to a clinical audience one of the most precious moments of his life.

"Tell me you didn't," Frank groaned.

"I made sure that Marta's first kiss was from someone she could trust with her life, someone who was willing to take a bullet for her." Matt looked Frank straight in the eye as he gave his answer, suddenly confident that he'd done the right thing. "I won't apologize for that. I do, however, apologize for disappearing with her. That was inexcusable. I am asking not to be removed from this case. You can fire me afterwards, but she needs me right now."

"You sound very much like a man in love," Frank stated flatly.

"I will do my absolute best to maintain professional decorum and to follow procedure. You should know that I will also do everything in my power to protect that young woman physically, emotionally, and spiritually. There you have it." Matt didn't flinch. If they fired him, he would continue to protect her on his own. He would not back away and leave her to wolves. He wasn't sure that was love, as Frank said, but that was the reality of the moment.

Frank gave a curt nod. "I'd like to talk this over with Rusty. Please give us a few minutes. I'll call you when we're ready to discuss our decision."

Matt's stomach tumbled to his toes as he left the room. The only bright spot was that his future was in the hands of two men he trusted. A verse came back to him about letting God do the fighting and just being still. He clung to that assurance and sat down to silently pray. Someone sat down next to him and Matt looked up to see Timothy Parsons. He couldn't think of anyone he'd less like to see right now.

"Hi," Timothy looked a bit uncertain as he greeted Matt. "You're in on the surveillance for this, huh?"

Matt nodded, thinking that he was for the time being anyway.

"I guess I'm going to be dating this dangerous lady." Matt glanced at him in surprise at his reference to Marta as dangerous. "It's sure going to be weird. It's like courting under the eyes of unknown chaperons." Matt gave him an amused look. He couldn't agree with him more. At least this guy had the chaperon's permission. That thought suddenly made Matt furiously jealous. Not for the first time, he wanted to punch this guy's lights out.

"You kind of like her, too, don't you?" The annoying Timothy broke into Matt's thoughts of violence against him, not decreasing his growing desire to do the man harm. "Hey, no offense intended, you know," Timothy obviously had picked up on Matt's nonverbal signals. "I think she sort of casts a spell over most guys. I'm nervous about falling for her myself. I mean, she's been kind of a fantasy for all us guys for a long time. Now she's a real person, maybe in a lot of trouble. It makes a guy want to be a knight in shining armor or something."

Matt glowered at him through slit eyelids letting him know he had properly interpreted the situation and might be better off elsewhere. The jerk evidently picked up on that, too.

"Well, I better finish up with the other agents," Timothy rose with a bit of a twitch that signaled to Matt how nervous he was.

Matt might cut him some slack, later. "They're planning things out for tonight." Nope the guy was getting no slack at all. He couldn't seem to keep from rubbing salt in Matt's wounds.

Matt nodded curtly as the guy scurried away. What seemed like an eternity, but was really a few minutes later, the door at the end of the hall opened. Rusty signaled him to come in. Frank stood looking out the window but turned as Matt entered.

"You're still on the case," Frank said briskly, "if I can convince the military that your bond with the subject is too powerful to replace at this point. But you screw up one more time and you are off the case. I will issue a letter of caution for formal addition to your personnel file if you force me by your actions to remove you from this case. Are we clear?"

Matt nodded, swallowing hard. This was not easier because it came from one of his best friends. He knew it was harder on Frank. "I will do my best, Frank," he responded, totally humbled.

Frank's face softened, "That's all we can ask. That's all we can ask of anyone."

Frank turned to Rusty, "You two get in on the planning session for the 'date' tonight. Jim and Verna will be in the surveillance van. We'll leave the surveillance stuff on automatic next door to her apartment. I think external surveillance will be sufficient. For the date, what do you think of a double date for the first time out, Rusty? Think we could sell it?"

"It would be a sensible safety net for a first date with someone you just met. In this specific case, we're dealing with a first date ever?" Rusty turned to Matt for confirmation. He nodded curtly since he couldn't get any words past the lump in his throat. It was Marta's first date, and he couldn't take her on it.

Rusty continued, "I think there will be no problem convincing Marta. Jane would love to get all dressed up and go out on the town. We might have a rough time with the young gentleman in there. He's got visions of Sir Lancelot dancing in his head. I'd like to slow him down a bit."

"Agreed then," Frank said decisively, "Rusty, you do the convincing with our young Romeo. I don't think he'll take it from Matt."

"No," Matt agreed, "he spoke with me a little in the hall and I'm afraid he's picked up on my attraction to Marta. Sorry I haven't kept it under wraps better. At least the bad guys ought to believe my cover, huh?" Matt grinned wryly. Frank laughed outright and clapped him on the back, breaking the tension between them.

"Okay, little brother," Rusty grinned, "let's get to work on Romeo's date."

They left Frank's office and joined two other agents with Timothy Parsons back in the conference room.

"Are we set on the Silverdale Hotel for dinner? Stay for dancing after?" Verna was recapping as they came in. Timothy was nodding in agreement.

"I have a curve to throw you, Timothy," Rusty broke in with his typical wise guy grin. "How about a double date with my lovely 'bride' and me?" Timothy looked totally blank. "Hi, my name is Rusty O'Hara. I'll be your pilot on this flight into the netherworld of espionage, spy, and counter spy routine." The other agents groaned, knowing that the irrepressible Rusty wit was unleashed without possibility of retrieval. Timothy continued to look blank but managed to hold out his hand for Rusty's hearty hand shake.

"My 'bride' refers to the female agent you saw with Marta last night at the bar," Rusty continued his comedy routine. "She's with Marta as we speak, shopping for the mega-date tonight. We thought a double date might work really well since Jane probably couldn't resist buying a new outfit that her real husband will have a cow about unless the FBI pays for it as an undercover expense."

Verna rolled her eyes, shaking her head as she responded to the shopping jab, "The boys always think us girls get compensated for any shopping we do undercover. That is so not true. We either have to turn it in or pay for it. What the government pays for, the government owns."

"As I was saying before being so rudely interrupted," Rusty gave Verna an exaggerated scowl, "we thought a double date would work very conveniently for a cover. It would be natural for friends to worry about a first date with a stranger. What's difficult here is that the friends only met her one night before you, the stranger, met her. Jane, however, has established herself as the motherly type…if you tell her I said that I will vehemently deny it. We, as a 'family', have established ourselves as Christians who take more than a passing interest in our new neighbor. She gave her life to the Lord under surveillance this morning. We've rejoiced and admonished under surveillance, thus establishing a sort of spiritual parent relationship. By the way, if anyone is wondering, that was all very real, unplanned, and totally sincere on all hands. We will continue, after this mess is over, to view that young lady as a spiritual daughter," he fixed a stern stare on Timothy.

"You are kidding, right?" Timothy's stare went from blank to amazement. Matt was trying very hard not to laugh out loud.

"Not a bit of it." Rusty replied gaily. "You'd better treat her very nicely and no hanky-panky. Papa is watching."

"Do you mean to tell me," Timothy finally laughed, releasing everyone else in the room to finally give in, "that I've traded in the Arctic Queen for a couple of evangelical FBI agents? What did I do to deserve this?"

"Well, for one, you work for a senator who got targeted by some sort of KGB look-alike criminal or terrorist group that have stuck their nasty heads up from beneath whatever rock they've been hiding under so we can nab them. Second, you've treated a beautiful young woman like a trophy instead of a person. But enough of personalities, on to the plan," Rusty's irrepressible humor, Matt noticed, had taken the bite out of his words and the tension out of the room. "I like the idea of dinner and dancing at the Silverdale Hotel. I know Jane won't be too tired from helping Marta spend all that spook money. Nothing energizes a woman like spending someone else's money. By the way, those bills are marked aren't they?" Rusty addressed Jim, who'd be manning the surveillance van that night.

"We traded out the spook money and gave some marked bills of our own. The serial numbers on the spook money are being traced right now. They're probably well laundered, though," Jim replied.

"Ah, the tricks they play on us," Rusty grinned at Timothy again. He had succeeded in making the young man totally comfortable with him. Matt had seen it a hundred times, but was still amazed at the people skills Rusty exhibited. "So, Tim, we'll be ready at what time?" Rusty batted his eyelashes, hamming up the comic aspects of the situation. They decided on 7:00 and broke up the meeting just in time for Rusty and Matt to meet the ladies back at the apartment complex.

Matt saw them first, loaded down with packages, heading for the stairs from their car. He was glad to note Jane's alertness. She'd spotted him right away.

"Hey, guys, not a bad haul, huh?" Jane shouted up the stairs.

"Looks great," Rusty bantered back, taking some of her packages as Matt relieved Marta of some of hers, "as long as it's all Marta's." He tried to look stern, but that was not Rusty's best look.

"Well, I did have to pick up a little something," she answered tentatively. "After all, it was on sale." She over did the innocent look a bit.

Rusty sighed, giving Matt a long suffering look and getting no sympathy, "Bit in the wallet again. We can't leave them alone for a minute. All right. Since you bought something new, I propose you have somewhere to wear it. Marta let you spend money after I expressly warned her not to, so we're going to horn in on her date tonight."

Jane's look of satisfaction signaled Matt that she'd been thinking along the same lines. "Marta and I were just discussing that," Jane answered as they headed up the stairs. "Marta only met this guy last night, though she's seen him around at races for years. We were a little concerned about the wisdom of her going out alone with a virtual stranger. I think a double date is just what the doctor ordered."

"I'd really like that," Marta added softly, with a look of regret toward Matt. He grinned at her ruefully.

"Great, you guys all go have fun while I get dishpan hands working behind the bar tonight," Matt groused as he gave them his most pitiful hang dog look. He got a laugh from Marta for his clowning. The sound was sweet. He wished this was all over so he could devote most of his time to evoking that sound.

Marta couldn't help gloating over her purchases as she put each garment carefully away. She was so glad Jane had thought of buying nice new undergarments to go with them. She felt the fabrics as she studied her now crowded closet trying to decide what to wear on her very first date. How she wished it could have been with Matt. She slipped, just for a moment, into the daydream that their relationship was normal. She relived the bliss of the afternoon kiss. She had felt cherished and protected. She belonged to him as surely as any woman ever belonged to a man, and he belonged to her. She had no doubts in this wonderful fantasy moment. A sharp knock at her door ended her dreamy thoughts and brought her back to the present.

Jane stood there, sparkling with excitement in her new moss green dress. "What do you think? Why aren't you dressed yet?"

"You look beautiful. I was daydreaming," Marta sheepishly admitted. Jane's eyes softened with a look of understanding. Marta wondered how obvious it was that she'd rather be going with Matt tonight and how much he'd told the other agents about their afternoon disappearance. She knew he probably had to give an explanation. "No more time for that, though. I need someone to help me decide what to wear or I'll spend all night in my closet!"

Like two giggling teenagers, they went through garment after garment and finally decided on a deep rose sheath with an inlay of rose lace at the breast. It was sleeveless, so she got to add a light weight jacket which exploded in a multicolored cloudburst pattern. Jane pulled Marta's hair up into a plush satin banana clip that matched her dress. The effect was a cascade of curls down her back.

They had bought some make-up that afternoon at the mall. Marta watched in the mirror, fascinated as Jane touched here and dabbed there working a subtle magic. The effect was spectacular. Marta felt like a fashion model or a movie star. She noticed that Jane had worked the same magic on her own face, bringing out the deep brown of her eyes and softening her lip lines with color.

"When I have more time I'll teach you some tricks," Jane winked. "Those of us, who, unlike another person in this room, were not born beautiful, have to learn the artistry of face paint early on."

Marta had no idea how to respond. "I…I really like how you've made me look. I like how you look. I always think you look lovely."

"Of course you do, and well you should. I do look lovely. God's love does wonders for a plain face like mine and without make-up too. Right? Right! Now let's go show the boys how gorgeous we are."

Marta could hardly wait to see how Matt would react. Would he like her all dolled up?

The scent of exotic perfume warned the gentlemen that the ladies were on their way.

"Now, Matt," Rusty's fatherly tone warned Matt advice was about to follow, probably hilarious advice that it was better not to take; "be sure and go gaw-gaw over these girls or we'll never hear the end of it. You must notice how lovely they are, but you must never notice the make-up no matter how thick they lay it on."

"Right," Matt tried to look serious as the door knob turned. Once the ladies entered, he forgot Rusty's advice. He forgot Rusty. He forgot his own name and what planet he was on. The queen of his heart had entered and he was lost. She took his breath away. As beautiful as she had been before, with her hair falling in her face, old grubby clothes, and not a speck of make-up, she was now a vision. No one was safe. Reality intruded as he remembered that all this care and preparation was for another man. Matt hadn't thought he could hate as thoroughly as he hated Timothy Parsons at this moment. He tried to release it all to the Lord, but it seemed compacted somewhere in the middle of his chest.

Marta studied Matt's face to see if he liked the effect. At first he seemed pleasantly blown away, but a sudden scowl sent another message. What had she done wrong? "Do you like my dress?" she asked shyly, hoping to get some kind of response to explain what was wrong. "This is the one you helped pick out."

"Don't rub it in," he growled back at her. His tone sliced through Marta like a knife. If she hadn't stood her ground through years of Peter's constant criticism, she would have fled in tears. She steeled herself to endure this evening, whatever it took. She had a job to do and it didn't include pleasing Matt Barton's fashion sense or any of his other senses.

Rusty hooted, "The old green-eyed monster has got my little brother-in-law by the throat. Yes indeed. This is going to be a very long night."

"Again," Matt turned to Rusty and spit through clenched teeth, "don't rub it in."

"Enough, you silly boys," Jane warned, "tell us how gorgeous we are or I promise I will burn dinner for the rest of your unnatural lives."

"You are both ravishing," Rusty clowned. "Never have I seen such gorgeosity, and I, my friends have been in a position to observe. I have been to Rodeo Drive."

"Give me a break," Jane mugged at him. Marta saw Matt start to soften and look somewhat sheepish under the teasing.

"You both look very nice," Matt's tone of concession was not all that Marta dreamed it would be, but she'd take it. She needed a little confidence to get through this awful date.

Rusty sidled up to Marta, "He's just mad 'cause he doesn't get to go and I do." Rusty gave Matt a sidelong look, "You ladies both look beautiful. Yes you do, and lucky is the man who gets to escort you two lovelies on the town. I regret having to share the loveliness, but I do not regret sharing the bill."

No one could help laughing at Rusty. He'd succeeded in breaking down the tension just in time. Marta's date arrived to the sound of their laughter. Rusty covered with another joke, keeping all hint of Matt's earlier reaction out of it.

Marta didn't have time to tense up again before Rusty was ushering them out the door as he explained the presence of another couple on his date. "That hotel on the bay is a nice place and close by. What do you say to that for the evening Tim? Oh, by the way, we're Marta's neighbors and we don't know you very well so we decided to tag along on your date and cramp your style."

Timothy stared blankly at him for a moment, and then burst into laughter. "I have no idea who you are, but you're all right. Anybody who can have me laughing while they ruin my whole evening is someone I must get to know. I work in Washington D.C. and making people laugh while you do them in is a talent I would like to learn."

"I'm Rusty, Jane's husband. You met Jane when you met Marta and you'd better remember her. Women are really sensitive about junk like that."

"What makes you think you know anything about women's sensitivities," Jane came back at him. The teasing banter continued in that vein as they walked the few blocks to the hotel restaurant. Marta was glad she'd followed Jane's advice and bought comfortable shoes.

CHAPTER ELEVEN

As they entered the hotel, Marta felt engulfed by its elegance. Its muted mélange of lavender, beiges, and aqua soothed her somehow. They were early enough to get a window table and enjoy the panoramic view of Dyes Inlet. A waiter asked them for their drink orders. Rusty suavely established a non-alcoholic evening, so Marta was relieved of another anxiety. Timothy shared a joke with her about their penchant for designer water.

To Marta's surprise, there was a photographer working the room. She'd never eaten here but was pretty familiar with which clubs and restaurants used freelance photographers to provide souvenir photos for their patrons. She had done very little of that work, but she kept informed. This hotel had never had one before. Then it occurred to her that the photographer was an FBI plant.

"Would you like a souvenir picture?" the photographer asked pleasantly.

Timothy looked quizzically at Marta. She nodded in the affirmative. Maybe it was dumb, but this was her first date. Rusty and Jane firmly declined. It occurred to Marta that they didn't want pictures floating around tying them too closely with this case. Too late, Peter probably had his walls plastered with pictures of them by now. The photographer snapped their picture.

Marta began studying her menu, feeling exhilarated by being able to order whatever she wanted. After all, this guy could afford it.

"Has everyone decided?" the waiter broke into her thoughts and she looked blankly around the table. They were all looking at her! She looked at Timothy.

He leaned toward her, "Would you like me to order for you?" he asked softly.

"Ah, yes, please. Some sort of fish, okay?" She looked apologetically at the waiter. "There's so much on the menu...."

He laughed politely. Marta was sure she'd been totally gauche, but what did it matter? After all, there were only a few hundred people witnessing this date. Timothy seemed inordinately pleased that she didn't even have brains enough to order her own dinner. Jane winked at her across the table as if she'd just won a major coup. Maybe having the guy order was all right.

When the meals came, she was glad Timothy had ordered for her. It smelled heavenly. She was about to take her first bite when she saw Rusty and Jane quickly and quietly bow their head over their meals. She, too, bowed over the savory smells. She didn't know what to say, so she just thanked Him for this wonderful food. Timothy handled it all with the grace of a polished politician, smiling as they raised their heads.

"A *Santé*," he saluted with his fork and took the first bite. "Mmm, this is as good as it gets."

"The steak is great, too," Rusty grinned. "I've got good taste in restaurants. I'm glad you asked us out."

Timothy guffawed, "I don't remember asking you!"

"Well, it's a package deal, isn't it? Ask girl, ask her over-protective, nosy neighbors," Rusty shot right back.

"I, for one," Jane cut in, "am not nosy."

"Oh, right, sure. Like I suggested we should chaperon."

"Like you most assuredly did. 'She doesn't know him,' you said. 'She met him in a bar,' you said. 'He could be an ax murderer,' you said."

Marta was laughing so hard she had tears running down her cheeks. Timothy gave her a disparaging look and plowed into the discussion.

Turning to the laughing Marta, he asked seriously, very seriously, "Do you think I'm an ax murder?" His eyebrows were practically raised into his hair line. Marta couldn't stop laughing long enough to verbalize so she shook her head in the negative.

As soon as she got her breath, she said, "No, you look like a guy in custom running shoes who's gonna get left in the dust next Saturday by a gal wearing sale rack Nikes with a few thousand miles on them."

"Ah ha," Rusty crowed, "a challenge if I ever heard one."

Timothy turned back to her with one eyebrow raised in the Vulcan salute, "I never, ever compete with a beautiful woman. Of course I don't let them win either."

"*Let?*" Jane's body language screamed challenge. "Have you seen her run? There will be no *letting* here. *Let* my right foot."

Marta had broken up again and couldn't speak. She couldn't remember ever laughing so much before in her life. She blessed Rusty and Jane for breaking the ice for her this way.

Timothy just looked at Jane through eyelids closed to slits, "You two really must stop long enough to allow this poor young woman to eat a bite or two of her delicious grilled salmon before it gets cold."

Jane and Rusty looked at each other with deadpan expression, and then took on a look of ultra sophistication. Rusty turned to Marta with, "Yes, my dear, do taste your fish." He and Jane then gleefully began eating their own meal as Marta tried to stop laughing long enough to eat. When she did, the salmon was worth the billing it received, even if it had gotten a little cold. The waiter offered a dessert tray filled with lovely things, but they were all too full. They promised each other they'd come back one day just for dessert. Marta caught the photographer snapping their pictures again as they left. It struck her as odd, but she didn't worry about it as they entered the club. The music was just starting.

Marta had never frequented clubs or taverns and the smell of stale alcohol overpowered her. She hoped her sensitivity to the awful smell would lessen as the evening wore on. She requested a glass of sparkling water when the waiter took their order.

Rusty and Jane had another boisterous comedy routine going on, and the waiter had to interrupt them to get their order. All the orders were non-alcoholic. The waiter explained that a designated driver would receive non-alcoholic beverages free if the others ordered alcoholic drinks.

Rusty laughed, "This is what we're like sober! I don't think your establishment could survive us tipsy, much less drunk."

Timothy entered the teasing, "The lady," he inclined his head toward Marta, "and I have a race next Saturday. She has threatened to run me into the ground. I'm taking no chances that she makes good on that threat so I am officially in training." The waiter laughed and went to get their drinks.

"So," Marta grinned, "you've picked up the gauntlet. I want you to know I'm not holding back next Saturday. I'm going for the gold." Marta felt exhilarated at the thought of running to win. She'd always held back to avoid drawing attention to herself, but now she had so much attention that one little first place wasn't going to make any difference at all. Her excitement was dampened by the reaction she saw in Timothy. Evidently he found the idea of running all out against her exciting too. His nostrils flared; his eyes glittered. He was excited, but she didn't like how excited and why. She suddenly felt like a rabbit seeing the shadow of a hawk soaring above her head.

Rusty rescued her by asking her to dance. Everyone laughed at his look of triumph for stealing the first dance from Timothy.

As she made her way to the dance floor with Rusty, Marta heard Jane goading Timothy, "Come on, we can't let them get away with this. Let's go show those two how it's done."

The music was good and Marta hardly sat down all night. When Timothy or Rusty weren't dancing with her, someone else was. Timothy had gotten a little gruff a couple of times when too many guys tried to cut in on him. Rusty had cut in once when one of the guys danced a little too close for comfort. Marta felt well protected between the two of them. They must have spent a fortune on sparkling water to slake their thirst after all the exercise the dance floor afforded. The whole place seemed focused on the rollicking good time they had together until, amazingly, the last set was played and it was time to go home.

Rusty and Jane disappeared discreetly into their apartment and left Marta to face Timothy alone for the first time. She hadn't the slightest idea what to do. Fortunately, Timothy did.

"Thank you, Marta," he said softly, "for one of the most memorable evenings I've ever enjoyed."

"A good bit of that had to do with my choice of chaperones, don't you think?"

"You bet. They sure beat the Arctic Queen...." Timothy suddenly looked as if he wanted to rip his own tongue out.

"The Arctic Queen?" she asked, raising her left eyebrow and narrowing her eyelids to slits. She didn't like the sound of this at all.

"I'm sorry Marta. That's what we called the lady you used to run with."

"My mother? Who's *we*?" She shot back. Fury began to build within her at this smug, good looking guy and whoever "we" turned out to be.

"The guys, you know, the guys I run with," Timothy stammered, his face turning several shades of red.

"Ah, now I know," she nodded, the light slowly dawning. Men stared at her not because she was strange but because of that strange excitement she's seen in Timothy earlier that had made her feel hunted. "You're one of those guys...one of the guys who stare at me for no apparent reason...one of the guys who make up funny nicknames for women...one of those guys. I understand, now, believe me I do. My mother obviously understood too. Forgive me if I don't invite you in. Good night, Mr. Parsons." She turned her back on him and unlocked her door to a litany of apology from Timothy. She was shaking with fury and humiliation. Without the buffer of Jane and Rusty, she could no longer handle the raging emotions.

She shut the door in Timothy's face, glad to be rid of him. She wanted Matt. She went to the kitchen and found some left over 7-Up. It was flat, but she drank it anyway. She found some soda crackers and was munching furiously when she realized that someone was knocking at her door. She felt a sudden flair of intense hope that it was Matt until she heard Jane's voice softly calling her name. She went numbly to answer the door. She wanted Matt, not Jane. But Jane was here, and Marta would take whatever comfort she could get.

"What happened?" the motherly voice asked as she held her and stoked her hair.

"Timothy told me that they called Tanya, my mother, the Arctic Queen. They were a bunch of runners who were at all the local races, a kind of clique. They were the 'cool' guys, you know, the ones everyone else copied. It seemed like once they got it started, I got smirked at by every male in running shorts in the Pacific Northwest. When he told me they had some had some stupid name for Tanya, I just got so mad. When I was a teenager, they made my life miserable by staring at me and snickering. They haven't been much better since. I thought there was something horribly wrong with me. I didn't understand until tonight that they were on the hunt. I know that individually they are probably really nice, but together they were like a pack of wolves and I was the prey. I hate that feeling."

"It's okay," Jane soothed. "It's natural to feel angry when someone touches an open wound, Honey. You calm down now and think about things. Old Tim isn't a bad guy, Marta, really. All guys are clods when they get in a group like that."

"Was Rusty ever like that?"

"All guys are like that sometimes. It's a part of who they are and how they relate to each other and to us. It's not personal, and it's not really dangerous most of the time. It's not pleasant for us, and it's not nice. I'm not excusing it, mind you, and neither does Rusty. He and Matt are both gentlemen in every sense of the word. They learned that at Christ's feet, though, and Timothy doesn't seem to have that tremendous advantage in understanding the needs of women."

"But Jesus was a man, Jane? How could He understand what we need as women?"

"Read the first chapter of the Gospel of John. It says He made everything. That means He made women, too. He knows how we tick, even when we don't know ourselves. You can also check all four of the Gospels in the New Testament and see how He treated women when He was on earth. In a culture where women were property, He invariably treated them as individuals with their own personhood, always with respect and courtesy. He understands us, Honey, and He explains to the men who have given themselves to Him how they are to treat us. Some obey better than others, I must admit, but we're all in process. God's not finished with any of us yet."

Marta lifted her head from Jane's shoulder and looked into her eyes to see if she really meant all this. Marta had never thought in such terms before. She saw only sincerity and tenderness in those clear brown eyes.

"Feeling better?" Jane asked.

Marta nodded with a sheepish little smile. "I'm so sorry. You must be exhausted. You didn't know what you were getting into when you moved in next door to me."

"I feel honored that you've turned to us, Marta. Not everyone would be as open as you've been. You've taken tremendous emotional risks with us. We want you to know that we cherish your trust and intend to be worthy of it."

Marta nodded again and, stepping away from Jane's hug, found herself swaying with fatigue.

"Get to bed," Jane commanded. "Remember, it's your turn to cook breakfast tomorrow!" Marta laughed, relishing the friendship that surely couldn't all be a cover.

CHAPTER TWELVE

Marta awakened from the sweetest dream of strong arms and safety to the almost smothering smell of stale alcohol. She reluctantly let go of her dream and wondered if she could redirect this dating thing from bars in order to avoid the severe headache sleeping with that smell in her hair gave her. A shower and a good run would clear the headache.

Matt was just coming out in running shorts as Marta left her apartment. She felt a bit awkward. This was the first time they'd been alone with each other since she'd asked him to kiss her. She blushed as she remembered the sweetness of that moment.

"I didn't know if you'd make it after your wild night out last night," Matt grinned, breaking the ice.

"Too true. I'm not used to these late hours, but we working stiffs just have to bite the bullet and get up. Besides I missed my run yesterday."

"Yeah, one day off is enough. Let's do it."

With that they took off at an easy warm-up pace. They hit the main drag with its traffic noise, and Marta fell into a comfortable rhythm and lost all sense of discomfort with Matt. It was good to feel her muscles moving her smoothly through the fresh morning air and the soft patter of rain. She looked over at Matt, and he gave her a comradely grin. It was good to be together again. Marta savored that. As they made the turn to take the last half of their route, ending at the apartment complex, Matt began a short briefing.

"Go about your normal routine today. I understand you need to work at a print shop today?"

"Yes, I work a couple of days a week in the photo and print shop for Al so he can have a couple of days off. The mall requires the store be open 7 days a week. He also has equipment I can use to do larger prints for customers who want posters and I print brochures for my customers there because he has a professional quality printer. I get an employee discount that improves my profit margin."

"Timothy Parsons is going to try to get in touch with you today or tomorrow. You're to respond positively even if he is a complete jerk."

Matt's excessively pleased expression gave Marta the impression that he liked it that she had slammed her door in Timothy's face the night before.

"Okay, I will do my patriotic duty but not one bit more. That guy...I just got so mad. Did you know that group of goons he hangs around with are always staring at me? I thought I had two heads, or worse, that they knew something about me. They've made my life miserable at races. I didn't figure out until last night that they stare because I am their prey, and they're hunting."

Matt threw back his head and laughed a deep laugh. "Yes, that's an apt description. Jane said you were great, really great. But you really didn't know they were ogling you?"

"No. I thought there was something wrong with me all the time. I learned over the years to force myself to ignore them."

"Well, I'm just glad I never tried to ogle you. You'd take me out." He gave her a dumb look that she assumed was his "I'm so scared" look. She gave him a disparaging look in return and kicked in to her run. He spurted after her until he was next to her. They raced, full out, to the complex and stopped short as they saw Timothy Parsons, complete with the requisite dozen red roses waiting for them on the stairs.

"Oh darn," Matt said between puffs as they slowed to a cool down pace.

"Be nice," Marta rejoined and trotted toward her assigned task.

"Good morning," Timothy said to Marta, totally excluding Matt. "Please accept my apology and this little token to make up for my behavior last night."

"For me?" Matt chimed in and grabbed for the flowers much to Marta's amusement and Timothy's dismay. "Why, you shouldn't have."

"Buzz off, Bartender, I'm talking to the lady," Timothy growled and Marta noted that the unfortunate gentleman seemed to have no sense of humor this morning. "Please, Marta," he continued seriously, "I truly apologize for myself and all my friends. I really want to see you as much as I can while I'm here. I have an important black-tie fund raising dinner this weekend in Seattle and I was hoping you would go with me." He gave her a winsome smile.

"I accept your flowers, Timothy. They are lovely. I also accept your dinner invitation because I happen to have the most stunning new dress and I'm dying to wear it. Matt can't buzz off; however, because we're heading to the apartment he shares with his sister and her husband. I'm going to cook breakfast this morning because it's my turn to cook. Would you care to join us? You won't have to cook until tomorrow morning because the first time you get to be a guest. Right, Matt?" Matt simply glowered at Timothy and the growing silence became uncomfortable.

Luckily Jane came to the rescue. "Are you three going to stand on the steps and frown at each other all day, or are you coming to breakfast? We're getting hungry up here, and our cook is on the stairs!"

Marta laughed and ran up, forcing the two belligerent males to follow her. Rusty looked up guiltily from a bowl where he had obviously started scrambling eggs. "Hey!" Marta cried in mock horror, "It's my turn to poison you, Rusty. Give."

"Poison! Poison! Is that gratitude for the wonderful breakfast I prepared for you? I can't help your delicate and maidenly stomach."

"Where's your microwave?" Marta asked perplexed.

"Microwave? We cook food here; we don't nuke it," Rusty announced haughtily. Marta assumed the look on her face brought on the laughter from the rest of the group.

"You mean," Marta did not have to feign amazement, "you fried the eggs I ate yesterday?"

"Of course, in bacon grease. How else do you cook eggs?" Rusty seemed genuinely perplexed.

"Well, they tasted really good, but fried food always makes me sick. I just can't take it. Was the burger at the tavern fried, too?" Marta turned to Matt.

"In good old grill grease, Hon." He grinned, teasing, but Marta felt a deep thrill at his endearment.

"Well, sorry folks, I really do have a maidenly stomach. It can't do fried. I get a bad stomach every time." Marta felt better, having explained the continual stomach problems she'd had. Stress could have contributed, but she had really been getting worried. Jane looked relieved as well. "If you'd like to adjourn to my place, I'd be glad to nuke this stuff over there. Unless someone objects to nuked eggs?"

"No problem," Jane answered giving Rusty an extremely telling look. He raised one eyebrow in silent comment and agreed to join them as they paraded next door with their bowl of half beaten eggs. The breakfast proceeded merrily, with Timothy prepared for the grace. When Rusty explained Family Altar, though, it was just too much for Timothy, and he politely declined, citing a prior engagement. Marta felt guilty that she was relieved he'd left. She had been a stranger when these folks had shared their worship and study with her. Now she was reluctant to share it with Timothy. Somehow she knew that sharing her new faith was as necessary as breathing. She just wished it would come as naturally as it had with these three dear people. She looked fondly around at them, glorying in this intimacy, an intimacy that was even now being recorded and would be analyzed by how many strangers? She didn't care. These were proven friends even if they were FBI agents doing their job. She trusted them with her life. No one could get much closer than that.

"Interesting," Nicolai commented to Tanya. "This Parsons did not stay."

"He's the target, Nicolai. I'm sure of it. I have the run-down on him."

"You ran him through the embassy? What if whoever is interfering with us is tipped by that?"

"What's to tip, Nicky? They know we know. They meant for us to know. They're sweating us out, trying to get us out in the open, making mistakes."

"I've swept this place but don't see how they could have us bugged. Unless they've done what I've done," he nodded toward his directional surveillance monitor.

"Nicolai, I have the information. If they know I have it, they know. Do you want to know who this Parsons creature is or not?"

"Patience, My Dear. I'm an old man."

Her loud "Pah!" let him know what she thought of that.

"I am...getting old," he chuckled, knowing he was driving her crazy with his dawdling.

"We are all getting old. Me especially, waiting for you to get your mind around to where you'll listen to what I have for you."

"Tell, tell," he chuckled.

"Timothy Parsons is a senior aid to Senator Van Boren. Senator Van Boren is the power behind the war on drugs. Mr. Parsons is the son of Air Force Major General Avery Parsons. General Parsons is very much involved with certain military activities in Mexico. Would you care to put two and two together?"

"Somebody wants either to gain information or to discredit those two. We'll assume our nasty ex-colleagues have been hired by certain parties to do this. It makes sense. But why Marta? She's untried. Surely they can't know she's got the FBI hip deep in this thing. Not even madmen would walk right into such a trap. It would be suicide on several counts. And it must be someone who knows my connection with Marta and has some idea of my own activities."

"Chilling thought," Tanya responded.

"Indeed. Who could know so much and yet go undetected?"

Tanya took a deep breath, "Only someone we trust."

A deep sadness settled over Nicolai. Betrayal from within had always been a distinct possibility, but for so many years his people had been absolutely loyal. Yet. . .

"Tanya, no one in our network knows about Marta. Only three people know about the connection between Marta and me."

"But more than that know of Marta and that you were her control. More know that she has never been fielded."

"Why wait for me to activate her, though? Didn't Peter know the code?"

"No," Tanya grinned mischievously, "I never shared that bit of information with him."

Nicky was shocked. "How did you get away with such a thing?"

"I told him Moscow released it only to me with direction that only you and I were to have it. I explained to him that because of certain behavior of his which I felt it necessary to report to Moscow, there was some thought he would activate her for his own selfish purposes. He was not pleased. He tried once more to use his physical prowess against me and beat this weak little woman." She gave Nicolai a brief smile. "That was the night you came in time to keep me from sending him to a hospital. I think he appreciated your restraining me. I couldn't take any more of him by that time. I kept hoping Moscow would recall him so I could finish Marta's training on my own, but I guess they needed him there to watch me."

"Ah, yes, our paranoid friends had us so busy watching each other we really didn't have time to be very good spies did we?" Nicolai laughed, realizing even then that it could be gallows humor. His craft was broken. They probably knew about this apartment. Perhaps they knew of his many corporate identities and Swiss bank accounts. He had taken great risks to get necessary money to his army of entrepreneurs back home.

"So," the ever-practical Tanya began again, "we have Timothy Parsons which means this whole thing is probably linked to the Shatooni operatives who have joined with crime lords. They intercepted our meet with Marta, so they know who we are and what we are doing. We do not know if they are listening in. If they are, we're dead already, eh? Since we yet live, I assume they haven't been able to find us or they haven't broken through our scramblers. Brilliant invention.

"Frankly, My Dear, I'm just trying to stay alive."

"Anyway, it gets back to who knows enough to do this to us. Who knows enough about Marta? It could be beyond the circle of three but not far. They obviously know of the disappearance of certain files, but either aren't sure who has them or are trying to draw them out. Why else would Peter even mention them?"

"Good point. Ah, our group is breaking up their prayer meeting. I wonder if they're passing coded messages through their prayers."

"Whatever they're doing, they're very good at it. I don't think anyone could fake what we heard yesterday morning."

"Marta?"

"Yes, those few words were very telling. I think there was a real conversion yesterday and that the three FBI agents next door are sincerely very happy about it. I could be wrong. It's just. . . there's a quality to them that reminds me of others I have met. I was very grateful I never had to take on the particularly unpleasant duty of controlling the 'Christian menace' at home."

"Yes. I never understood such things. If you don't want to believe, why hurt those who do? What were they all so afraid of?"

"There is power in fear. Those who do not fear don't come under its power."

"Wise answer. Now let us focus that wisdom on who is trying to make us afraid and thus control us. It is, as you say, a small circle who could connect us with so many seemingly unconnected things. Who would know that Marta is part of our former KGB network and that you and I are the only ones who could activate her? Who would be able to keep track of both of us well enough to know our plans? We must follow this trail and hope that the files we have will give us the answers before harm comes to Marta or to us."

"Marta's leaving. Do you have someone on her, or should I go?"

"Let the FBI protect her for now. They are our best hope. You and I have work to do here."

Sergei Illyvich Polyev, code name Shatoon, stared balefully at the miserable excuse for a human being across from him. He had known this incompetent as Peter Alexander for so long that he couldn't even remember the man's real name. He sometimes wondered if Peter himself could remember it. Sergei looked over the innocent photos of lovely Marta and her target. They obviously were having a wonderful time. So were their busybody chaperons! He couldn't believe those pushy people actually went out on a date with a neighbor they'd known less than three days.

"These photos are a beginning," he barked at Peter, "but nothing without more compromising photos. She must entice him into a less innocent appearance, and she cannot do that with these meddlers from next door."

"You want me to take care of them?" Peter seemed to relish the thought of violence.

"No, not yet. We'll put the pressure on Marta to get alone with him. After all, she won't want her wonderful new friends hurt. No, no. They could be useful later on. We could use them against her should she drag her feet." Sergei nodded as he savored this new twist. The meddlers could be made to work to his advantage after all.

"So when do we do Gorgonov?" Peter asked impatiently. "I've been waiting a long time to get that old man back. He interfered with me once too often."

"In good time. We must please our Mexican customers first. Then you will see how we have Gorgonov right where we want him."

"I don't get how all of this is going to bring down Gorgonov."

"All in good time, my friend, you will understand all in good time."

"I know he has a soft spot for the girl, always has. You're going to use her to get to him, aren't you?" Peter leered at him.

How he hated being pumped for information. He decided to rid himself of Peter the minute he outlived his usefulness. The less this vermin knew the better. "Just get to the girl and tell her to heat up her relationship with her target or her new friends will suffer harm," he snapped. "Our colleagues to the South want the senator and the general discredited. Timothy Parsons photographed with the lover of a Mexican drug lord will accomplish just that. We'll get the most compromising photos we can of Parsons and the girl. Then she goes south to be a plaything. We'll ensure she gets as much media coverage as a Hollywood star for that role." Sergei laughed harshly, "That's all you need to know for now.

CHAPTER THIRTEEN

Matt felt a certain elation at being the one to accompany Marta to the photo finishing shop where she had access to high tech facilities. He'd been amazed that he alone had been assigned to her today. Well, they were not exactly alone. He groaned inwardly as he thought of all the eyes and ears that intruded on their privacy. How he would love to be truly alone with this woman, to have time to know her and the right to woo her.

"I sure hope I can get my processing done before the shop opens," Marta's anxious voice broke into Matt's thoughts. She opened the shop and stepped into strong chemical smells. Matt signaled her to wait and then went before her into the shop, checking it out for intruders. He nodded for her to come in.

"Nice set up," he commented, not really knowing anything about photography. It was just a bunch of smelly machines to him. He was a bit surprised when Marta passed up the fancy stuff out front and led him into a back room with a couple of sinks, some small metal tubes in a hand made rack off the side of one of the sinks, an old clothes line strung across one side with strips of film hanging from it, something that looked kind of like a copier with a couple of plastic bottles upended into it, and what reminded Matt very much of a huge microscope.

Marta turned to him with a grin, "Old fashioned, but it suits me fine. I don't use all that technology out there for the print media. I actually still use black and white film for those. That's why I change out cameras on the route. I use digital for color and either e-mail, print or post directly to web sites for digital media.

I use film for black and white prints that will go into newspapers and such. There's no replacing what you can do with light and shade in a good old fashioned black and white negative to sparkle on a newsprint page. I need to bring out the fine detail in the houses I take. I focus on the front door and have to set my aperture manually to ensure that detail, which is usually in shadow, is captured. I'll process this film and set it drying. I've got some left to print while the new stuff dries." She pointed to the strips of film hanging on the clothes line. "Please close the door and flip that switch over there. It'll shut off the lights in here but turn the red warning light on outside so no one will come barging in here and expose my film before I've got it developed. After that we'll go play with the toys out there for the poster sized enlargements."

Matt followed her instructions, and the room went pitch back. He felt enclosed in a tiny dark world with her. The intimacy set his heart racing, so he decided to concentrate on the process she was using rather than on her. He heard Marta moving around by the sink. Next he heard several strange noises that sounded like a wire whip, then a swishing noise, and finally metal sliding against metal.

Marta instructed him to turn the light back on. She set a timer and took some of the film off the line over to the big microscope contraption.

"This is my enlarger. I'll be transferring the picture from the negative to the print paper on this," she explained. "I'll need the light out again, but I'll use this light above the enlarger to give us a little light."

Matt watched fascinated as she loaded the film into the enlarger and a picture appeared on the paper below. She did something with a paper clip with a tiny piece of paper, waving it over the image, then ran the print through the machine that looked like a copier. Out came a picture of a house. She was setting the picture on a table when the buzzer from the timer sounded. She shut off all the dim lights, and Matt again heard still more metallic sounds from the pitch black. He heard her move again, and then, as if a fantasy come true, she ran right into him. His arms automatically closed around her, holding her to him. A breathless "Oh" sounded just below his chin, and he almost lost control. Her next words helped him regain it.

"I forgot you were there," she laughed unsteadily. "I'm so used to being in here alone; I just started to go over to turn on the light."

He had to let her go to turn on the light. His mind instructed his arms to let her go, but they just wouldn't. His head started lowering itself; his lips seemed to have a mind of their own as they started seeking hers.

"Matt?" her innocent query stopped him. He dropped his arms and reached for the light. The sudden glare blinded him, sparing him having to face her with the thought he was sure would otherwise have shown on his face. He sent up a prayer for strength. That had been very, very close.

Marta's eyes adjusted more quickly than Matt's, and she was again heading for the enlarger.

"You take advantage of every moment in here, don't you?" he asked noticing that his voice shook only a little.

"You bet. I get a limited number of hours a week and I can't afford to let any of it go unused. I also roll my own film here. That takes time and has to be done in complete darkness."

"You roll your film?"

"Sure. I buy it in 100-foot rolls and then break in down into 10, 15, and 20-shot rolls for my routes. It saves a lot so I can keep the price down and make up for the extra time these take. Most of my customers don't have a clue what it takes to get pictures that crisp and detailed in their print media marketing tools and they actually get more sales off the web sites. The good news is that my photos give them more return on their investment in print media, so it brings me more digital media customers as well.

There are enough folks still looking in newspapers and magazines for homes that realtors still use them."

Matt shook his head in amazement. He'd never thought much about photography before. He just took his pictures and dropped the film off, then picked them up an hour later. As a result, he'd never thought of photography as an art form. The artistry Marta brought to her photography blew him away.

Marta had him send them into pitch dark just one more time. When the buzzer went off again, she pulled a wire with several metallic coils holding her film out of the last metal tube at the sink. She hung it up, squeegeed it, and turned on a fan. She looked around and didn't seem to find what she was looking for.

"Darn, I was going to ask you to use my blow dryer on this film to hurry it through the drying process, but I don't see it here. Maybe I left it in the car. Would you mind moving the fan every few minutes while I go look for it?"

"No problem." Matt repositioned the fan, and she nodded her approval as she ducked out of the dark room.

As Marta approached her car, she was lost in a reverie of how good being in Matt's arms had felt. Just as she reached the door, a hand shot out and held it shut. She froze, the hair on her neck standing at attention. It was coming now. She'd let her guard down, and it was coming.

"Hello, daughter dear," the sneering voice of Peter assailed her and chills ran through her. "You're not very nice to your Mr. Parsons, are you? Did you really think you needed chaperons to do what I told you to do?"

"No, they just suggested. . . Jane has been so helpful. I mean, she was there when I met him. She and Matt helped me pick out clothes. I didn't know what to wear. I've never dated, Peter. I wouldn't have known how to act with Timothy without them. We double dated. I'd just met Timothy and in a tavern. They were being caring."

"Make sure they are less caring from now on," Peter ordered through clenched teeth. "This one in the dark room with you now, what is he about?"

"He's helping me with my film because I lost so much time yesterday shopping. You said to fix myself up, so I did. It took time. When this is over, I still have to make a living, you know. My customers are expecting their pictures to meet the newspaper deadlines this afternoon."

"Your concern now is to do what I tell you to do. Get rid of these people, or I will get rid of them for you, do you understand?" Marta froze in horror. He would hurt them. She hoped there was someone watching them now and recording this. Surely they would warn Jane and Rusty. She heard the door of the shop open behind her and her heart sank. Peter could kill Matt right now before anyone could get there to stop him. She had to do something. The last thing Peter would expect popped into her head. She reached up and kissed his cheek.

"Papa, Oh Papa, how did you know to find me here? It's so good to see you," she cried loud enough for Matt to hear, hoping he would get the message and follow her lead. Peter's shocked expression was priceless, but she would have to store it away to savor later, if she lived to have a later. She felt Matt come up behind them.

"Did you say 'Papa'?" Matt asked as Marta turned toward him.

"Yes, Matt Barton, please meet my father, Peter Alexander."

Matt held out his hand in greeting, and the dismayed Peter was forced to shake it.

"When did you get into town, Papa? How is Mamma? Is she with you?" Marta enjoyed watching Peter squirm. She'd forced him right into the spotlight, and he didn't like it one little bit.

"I just got in," Peter answered guardedly. "Your mother couldn't come with me this time."

Marta almost laughed aloud. He probably hadn't seen Tanya in years.

"Are you staying at the resort again? It's so convenient, just down the street really," Marta chattered on, determined to control Peter's movements. "I really wish Papa could stay with me, Matt, but you know I have no place for him in my small apartment. Matt and I were working in the dark room, and I really must finish. My customers are waiting, you know. Can you wait while we finish up and then we can visit, or do you have other business you must attend to?"

"I have other business," Peter ground out. "I'll have to see you later. I'll be in touch, I promise you."

"Oh, good. I hope we can have dinner together, but I have such a strange schedule any more. I'm doing exactly as you advised, Papa. I'm giving people a chance and getting out more. I'm even dating, aren't I, Matt? You'd approve. He's very important, a senator's aid."

"Yes, very good. I'll see you later," Peter said, backing away toward a black sedan behind him. Obviously this interview had not ended to his liking.

"Bye for now then, Papa," Marta said sweetly. "We really must get back to work now, Matt." She turned Matt and headed him back toward the shop. Once back in the darkroom, safe behind closed doors, she turned into Matt's waiting arms and clung to his strength. He tightened his arms completely around her, pulling her into his protection and warmth. He laid his cheek on her hair and held her. She gradually stopped shaking, and her tense muscles relaxed. Matt loosened his hold, and she looked up at him, smiling. The tenderness in his eyes almost unnerved her, but as she received it, it gave her strength. They were together. They could get through this together.

She mouthed, "Can we talk?" He shook his head in the negative, so she found paper and wrote out Peter's orders and his threat. Matt nodded. She destroyed the writing in the sink with chemicals and threw it in the hazardous waste receptacle.

"Well, I guess I'd better get back to work if I'm to have my photos ready today."

"Your dad seems like a nice guy. Do you think you'll get to see much of him while he's in town? I assume he's here on business."

"Yes he's here on business, and I don't know if that will leave him much time for me. We'll have to see, won't we?"

"Yes I suppose we will. You want me to keep moving this fan, or did you find the hair dryer?"

"Use the fan. I don't seem to be having much luck with hair dryers today," Marta answered, irony in her tone. Matt gave her an understanding look and went back to drying film.

When Marta was finished, Matt took her to the FBI apartment where she and Jane could work on identifying photos. He walked up to the Kitsap Mall and used a public phone to call in for instruction on how to handle the latest glitch. Rusty picked up and brought Frank in on a conference call.

"We got the orders and the threat on tape," Frank filled Matt in on what the FBI surveillance picked up.

"Yeah, it matches what Marta wrote in a note to me in the dark room, Frank," Matt answered.

"How's she doing?" Rusty broke in anxiously.

"She's pretty shaken, but, all things considered, she's holding up well. She and Jane are busily trying to get her photos identified to addresses and out to the local papers. Jane's going to stick with her until told otherwise. I was able to pass her a note warning her about things heating up."

"What do you think, Matt?" Frank asked. "You were on the scene. Do you think this guy poses a real threat? Should we call off the operation and go for what we've got? From what we heard the other day, it sounds like the major players were called back to Moscow."

"This guy's not working alone, Frank. Rusty briefed me on what we've got on him. He's nothing but a messenger boy. He couldn't even handle Marta. She had control of him just by calling him her papa. My thought is that he's on someone's leash, and he is very, very scared of that someone."

"He said Gorgonov got called in and was in disgrace. So someone's running him, but whom?" Rusty posed.

"Got me! You got any brainstorms, Frank?"

"What if Gorgonov isn't gone? Maybe he's still here and is running the show. Our little messenger was given the job of disinformation or was given disinformation. No matter, I agree with Matt. We've got a master mind somewhere because Peter Alexander is no rocket scientist. Someone is behind the curtain pulling the strings. If there is any way, we've got to keep the operation going," Frank gave his decision firmly.

"Okay, we'll be a little more careful," Rusty agreed. "Matt, head back home and let the ladies know we're still a road show. Frank, you want us to stick as close or back off a little?"

"Let's back off to give them a little more room but not much. We'll keep the heavy surveillance going. We'll keep some on you guys, too. Sorry to say, but you have become bait as well. Keep that in mind at all times and don't anybody play hero."

"Got it, Boss." Matt answered seriously.

"We'll have Marta and Timothy go out on their own now. There's no more excuse for Rusty and Jane to tag along."

"Ah, that's no fun," Rusty complained. "I think poor Marta's going to be bored to tears having to spend time with Timothy. The guy never has anything to say."

"That's because you didn't let him get a word in edgeways, according to Jane," Matt teased.

"The stories that woman tells," Rusty rejoined. "Make this tale bearer get back to work, Frank."

"It's time we all get back to work. One more thing, Matt, I want you to play up the jealous boyfriend. That will give us some cover for keeping someone close to her. Hopefully she can hold her people off with the excuse that you won't go away."

"No problem," Matt responded enthusiastically.

"Remember, you're jealous because the bulk of her attention goes to Timothy, Matt. No fights over the girl, right?"

"To quote Rusty, 'Ah, that's no fun.'" Matt laughed.

Frank groaned and signed off with Rusty laughing in the background. Matt hung up and checked the area for anyone who was too interested in him. He'd kept up a sweep during the conversation, but careful was the watch word from here on out.

When he got back to the apartment, Timothy was there. He wouldn't have any trouble playing the jealous suitor. He reacted in character to the cozy scene of Timothy helping Marta package her photos for delivery. Evidently, they were waiting for the go ahead from him that the operation was still on before heading out together on a delivery route. He closed the door behind him and nodded to them, picking up paper and pen. He wrote out the operation status in a few terse sentences and passed it to Jane. She gave him a wry look and passed it to Marta who seemed to take it in stride. She must have assumed that the operation would continue. She passed it to Timothy, who looked inordinately pleased that Marta was instructed to heat things up with him. Matt seethed inwardly but could do nothing, and Timothy knew it. This was really not fun.

After a brief conversation, Marta was gone.

"Well, Little Brother, isn't it time for you to eat and get ready for work? You have the happy hour shift tonight." Jane's eyes twinkled at him as she reminded him that he'd be stuck behind a stupid bar that night while Timothy Parsons was heating things up with Marta. He gave her a dirty look and went to fix himself a sandwich. Maybe he could pick up something at that tavern. He'd concentrate on that and maybe, just maybe, forget those big blue eyes.

Marta was uncomfortable alone with Timothy, but he seemed to be working very hard to charm her into relaxing with him. After they finished the last delivery, Timothy suggested dinner and a movie. That seemed like a good idea. They wouldn't have to talk during the movie, and afterwards they could talk about the movie.

"Sure, that sounds good," she smiled a tight little smile at him. He patted her arm in a reassuring gesture, and she felt a glimmer of liking for him.

Dinner was lively and fun. Timothy bought a paper, and they worked over the entertainment page until, after much mock fighting, finally chose a movie they could agree on.

They held hands in line as they waited to get their ticket, and Marta missed the feel of Matt's hand. Timothy put his arm around her as they watched the film together, and she ached for the feel of Matt's arms as they had held her in the dark room that morning. He linked his arm in hers as they left the theater together, and she yearned for the sense of protection she felt with Matt. If Timothy tried to kiss her, she thought she would scream. Desecrating the memory of that holy kiss with a charade would surely push her over the edge. She wondered if Timothy could sense that.

"Would you like to have a cup of coffee before we call it a night?" Timothy broke into her thoughts with a reprieve from facing that probable good night kiss at the end of the evening.

"Sure, but let's make it a decaf latté in deference to my severe need for sleep." They had no trouble locating their latté. The coffee craze had started in the Seattle area, so Silverdale was dotted with espresso stands, and every restaurant and bar had to serve it or die commercially. Marta lingered as long as her exhaustion would allow her and then decided that giving him a kiss would be worth getting some sleep.

There were no lights in the apartment next door. Marta felt a stupid disappointment that they hadn't waited up for her. Matt, she knew, would still be at work. Timothy was bringing her home fairly early for a Friday night. She unlocked her door and turned toward Timothy, bracing herself to endure his embrace.

"Good night, Princess," Timothy chuckled. "This old dragon won't eat you yet."

"I'm sorry, have I been terrible?"

"No, just nervous. You haven't dated much, have you?"

"No. I never had time for relationships."

"I know. Me, too. I've dated a lot but developing relationships has been tough. I'd really like to work at a relationship with you, though. It won't be easy because I'm only here for the race next Saturday and then back to the other Washington. I'm back and forth quite a bit though. Think we can work something out, Lovely Lady?" He reached up and cradled her cheek in his hand. That wasn't bad. Marta could live with that touch. She nodded into his hand. He rubbed his thumb across her lower lip, seemed undecided for just a moment, then abruptly dropped his hand and stepped away.

"Good night, Marta. Tomorrow night is that fund raiser in Seattle. May I take you?"

"Yes, that would be nice. What time shall I be ready?"

"I'll pick you up around 4:15 to make the 5:25 Bainbridge Island Ferry. I have to get there early to help set up. Dinner won't be until 8:00 so I'll bring a snack to share on the ferry. I'll see you tomorrow afternoon then. I'll call before I come."

She nodded and slipped into her apartment, waving good-bye. She waited quietly until she heard his car leave, then went and listened at the wall she shared with the FBI agents. Were they up? Surely someone was monitoring in there, but the lights were out. She longed for a good long talk with Jane but resisted the urge. There was no natural way to approach them when their lights were out, and besides, she could be putting them in danger. She decided that a long soak in the tub would be the best substitute for Jane's motherly company. While she was soaking, she heard Matt come home. She resisted the urge to throw on her robe, rush out, and throw herself into his arms.

She heard sounds of movement in the next apartment and then Jane's laugh. They must have all gone to the tavern tonight. Marta scolded herself for feeling abandoned, pulled the plug on her bath, and, stopping only long enough to dry off and pull on a night gown, fell into bed.

CHAPTER FOURTEEN

Marta shared the plan for the formal dinner in Seattle with Matt as they ran, and he assured her she'd have plenty of cover.

"Timothy gave us an itinerary of 'dates' up until race day," Matt explained. "Jane says your new wardrobe will be more than adequate."

Marta laughed, gladdened by his teasing. She wished she could share a special night with Matt. Would that ever happen for them? She wondered.

Jane took over after breakfast and devotions. "This is girl stuff," she explained seriously. "The two of you would only be in the way." The guys then made themselves scarce as Jane outlined what all had to be accomplished before a formal date. The main obstacle was a hair dresser.

"You've never had your hair done? Ever?" Jane was aghast.

"Are you kidding? I make enough to eat and pay the rent, and that's about it," Marta explained, amused. "I keep my hair trimmed. It's long enough that I can reach the ends myself."

Jane had a friend, however, who came all the way from Seattle to a hair dresser in the little Bremerton neighborhood of Manette. Her friend had an appointment that day which she reluctantly donated in response to Jane's pleading. Marta had to admit, the man was an artist with hair. He somehow managed to get her long unruly hair into uniform ringlets and arranged them to cascade over one shoulder to leave one ear and shoulder exposed. That brought up the necessity of earrings. Jane found the perfect ones in a jewelry store in the mall. Marta tried to balk at the price, but Jane explained carefully that one couldn't wear junk to a $5000 a plate political fund raiser. It wasn't done.

Finally, back at the apartment, Jane slowed down enough to allow Marta some lunch before they started on her make up. It was closing in on 3:30 when she was finally satisfied with Marta's look. Jane had done her nails earlier, and they were finally dry. They both breathed a sigh of relief. All that was left was getting Marta into the dress, and that wouldn't take long.

"I'd take a little nap, but it would ruin my hair," Marta groused. "Are there really women who go through this all the time?"

"Honey, some women go through this kind of elaborate stuff every day. I never could see how they found the time. They must get up in the middle of the night to get ready for work."

"Not me, I like the natural look. It's easier." They both laughed. They fixed tea and visited until time for Marta to dress.

Marta slipped the sparkling pink creation over her hair carefully. Jane handed her the earrings with the air of a surgical nurse handing a surgeon a scalpel. The earrings were perfect, sparkling with the color of her dress. Marta gazed into the mirror at a glamorous stranger. Jane handed her lipstick, then perfume, which she obediently applied. The doorbell rang, indicating that Timothy was right on time. Jane answered the door to give Marta an entrance.

Timothy's reaction was everything a woman could hope for. His jaw dropped; his eyes bulged; and he couldn't speak for a few seconds. Timothy was stunning in his tuxedo, but he still wasn't Matt, and it was all Marta could do not to hate him for it.

Timothy escorted her to his car and Jane waved them off like a doting mother sending kids off to the prom. People on the ferry gave them amused looks as they promenaded the passenger deck in their formal attire.

"We could have stayed in the car," Timothy grinned, "but I wanted everyone to see that I'm with the most beautiful woman in the Pacific Northwest tonight." Marta shook her head and refused to respond. She wasn't particularly interested in giving Timothy an ego boost, but she was glad not to be cramped in the car during the ferry ride.

Timothy handled the heavy Seattle traffic expertly and got them to the Edgewater Inn without any heart-stopping close calls. They found the banquet hall in a flurry of preparation. "I won't be much company for awhile," Timothy warned her as a large man with a flowing white head of hair and a politician's smile started toward them.

"The Senator?" Marta chuckled.

"The very same. Get ready to be welcomed into the fold."

"Tim, my boy, how did a scrawny pup like you merit the company of this ravishing beauty. My Dear, if I weren't twenty years too old, and, of course, married to the most wonderful woman in the world, I'd give Tim a run for his money," the Senator almost crowed with delight.

Marta couldn't imagine what was making him so happy. Surely he'd been briefed on this whole charade. She held out her hand in response to his greeting, murmuring a few meaningless words while she prayed he wouldn't mangle her hand in his vice-like grip.

Matt and Rusty monitored the surveillance screen from one floor above the banquet hall. Matt saw her the minute they entered the room. Marta was a vision even on a tiny black and white monitor screen. What must she be like in person? Matt almost groaned aloud but caught himself in time.

"Stop drooling, Matt," Rusty admonished. "Sure the girl is a vision, but you needn't be so undone about it." The dry chuckle following that inane remark almost cost Rusty his front teeth. Matt decided, however, to remain professional.

"Subjects have entered banquet room," Matt ground through clenched teeth into his hand-held radio to alert the agents working the room. He expected no answer. The agents wore ear pieces like the Secret Service so they would be indistinguishable from the Senator's security.

Matt, with Rusty cracking jokes at his side, watched as Timothy abandoned Marta to the ranks of those who had no assignment in the bustle of activity. He was proud of the grace with which she handled it. She simply floated, he could think of no other way to describe her movement, to the windows. She seemed to lose herself in what Matt knew to be a spectacular view of Elliot Bay. How he would love to share it with her. Someday, he promised himself, they would stand as she was standing now and share that view together.

It seemed an endless time to Matt that Marta waited patiently by that window. He checked other monitors, clowned with Rusty, and still she remained almost motionless by that window. She didn't show any sign of feeling awkward.

Marta drank in the view and dreamed that she and Matt were sharing it. She could almost feel his presence. As she watched the changing colors of sky and sea, the sun shining through clouds off distance mountain tops, she felt she was joining him in a song of praise to the One who created all that beauty. She knew so little about the Lord she had just given herself to. How she wished that it could be Matt who would help her learn.

Will the Lord give me the desires of my heart? She had read that somewhere in her new Bible. She could not remember the verses so she could go back there again, but snatches of her readings kept coming into her mind at the most appropriate moment. Perhaps that was the Holy Spirit Jane and she had talked about over tea this afternoon. Amazing that God Himself was now dwelling in insignificant Marta Alexander. Marta lost herself in that thought so completely she jumped when Timothy touched her elbow.

"Sorry I left you on your own so long," he apologized. "We're all set up now and I think the last crisis has been handled, at least for the moment. Let's sit until the guests start arriving and we have to mingle."

She and Timothy talked mostly about their mutual interest in running until people started trickling in and the Senator and his entourage formed their receiving line. Marta was so relieved that Timothy didn't have that duty. His job was to mingle with the guests and see to their needs until the dinner started. She plastered on a smile and made a good imitation of a Mercedes Benz hood ornament since it was patently obvious Timothy was displaying her as a status symbol. She saw other lovely women in the room being used in much the same way and accepted that this was her job for the night.

What little conversation she made usually centered on running or how she'd met Timothy. Marta was shocked at how much notice she had drawn in local races simply by trying to avoid any attention. She was asked numerous times why she seemed to pull back from winning or placing. She shrugged and said she didn't realize she'd been doing that. Everyone enjoyed the story of how they met; especially that Timothy had been reading a book while all the other guys were vying for her attention. Marta realized that she was casting herself as a woman who couldn't bear having even one man ignore her, but she didn't care. She had been playing a part so long, that one more wrong impression didn't bother her that much. She was a little troubled by the fact that she was bending the truth. She knew, however, that she couldn't tell the truth without endangering people, so she decided to do her best and hold on to the Lord. She hoped that someday she would be free to be honest and open with everyone she met. Keeping secrets was too great a burden.

Marta survived through the banquet. She enjoyed the food, endured the speeches, and met some truly nice people. She was, however, very happy when Timothy finally steered her toward the door. She fell asleep as they waited for the next ferry home and didn't wake up until Timothy shook her in front of her apartment building. Somehow, he managed to get her up to her door. He finally took the key and got the door open, laughing at her comatose condition.

"A girl can only take so much, Timothy," she muttered. "Was nice, though," she smiled up at him vaguely. "I got to wear my dress. Goodnight." He gently pushed her in the door.

"Don't forget to lock the door, Marta."

"I won't. Goodnight." She finally got her deadbolt to lock and made her way to the bedroom, slipped out of her dress, then collapsed. The next thing she knew, sunlight was shining in her bedroom window.

She groaned as she slowly woke up and looked at the clock. It was already ten, but it was Sunday. She had just decided to roll over and go back to sleep when a knock woke her completely. She stumbled to the door in her robe to find Jane awaiting her on the other side with a steaming cup of coffee.

"Hi, Sleepy Head. You want to go to church with us? You have about fifteen minutes to get ready, and I know you can dress and don your natural look in that amount of time. Besides I want to hear every detail of the dream date."

Marta groaned and reached for the coffee, motioning Jane in. After Jane was seated, she went to her bedroom to grab one of her new outfits from the closet. The new wardrobe was a great assistance to her need for a quick departure.

She joined with Matt, Rusty, and Jane as they praised God in a church that was close to the apartments. Marta felt like she was finally part of a family. The feeling of being joined with the people around her reminded her of the thoughts she had as she enjoyed the view the night before.

As they walked home from church, Rusty took advantage of the relative privacy of the busy street to brief Marta.

"We're just playing it by ear now. There was no activity that we picked up on last night. There were so many legitimate photographers at that function that anyone could obtain photographs. We can't figure out how any of them could be used against anyone. Now, we just play out the scenario and see what pops up. You continue seeing Timothy. If Peter shows up again and tells you to heat things up, just tell him you'll marry the guy and be a lot more valuable an information source. We'll see if that brings out a big fish. Who knows. If that kind of confrontation happens, we'll close in to protect you. So just relax and enjoy the trip, okay?"

Rusty's irrepressible grin brought an answering smile from Marta. "Okay. Relaxed and enjoying, Sir. Can I relax into a nap this afternoon, though? I'm dead on my feet."

Laughing, they returned to their respective apartments and enjoyed a quiet afternoon.

Marta moved like a zombie through the subsequent days, putting on a show of falling for Timothy while she ached for Matt. Although she and Matt still ran together every morning, she saw very little of Rusty and Jane, who were up and out very early in the morning now. Marta sorely missed the prayer and Bible study with them in the morning. She started having her own and knew they were having theirs individually as well. It helped knowing that. But she still missed the closeness, the family feeling. Matt hovered as much as he could in the guise of a jealous rival, but he could have very little contact. She knew there was a beehive of activity all around her, but for her and Timothy it was just a week of being together often. He even went with her on photo routes, and she wondered if he wanted to be her protector. She hoped not.

True to her assignment, she let Timothy kiss her and hold her, hoping that would be enough for Peter and whoever was his control. If Matt had never kissed her, Marta thought she would have enjoyed Timothy's kisses. He was very good at it, and the sensations were far from unpleasant, but that was it. There was no coming together, no joining. It was just pleasant sensations. That would never be enough for Marta.

No further contact was made as the week went by, and Marta was lulled into a sense of numbness. Her focus subtly changed as she prepared for the Whaling Days race and festivities on Saturday. Timothy would be fun to share those things with, but Matt would be earth shaking. She hoped he would be at the race. She just wanted to run next to him as they did each morning. It was the closest they had been able to get.

"Nicolai," Tanya's urgent voice brought Nicolai in from the kitchen where he had been fixing yet another cup of tea. He entered the living room to find Tanya holding a file with a look of horror on her face. She looked up at him, and he saw anguish in her eyes as she held the file out to him. He took it with a sense of impending doom. He read the name Sergei Illyvich Polyev, his friend from early childhood, a friend who had loved Anna with him and grieved her loss with him and searched out her daughter with him. He was the only one besides Tanya who knew the whole truth, the only one who had experienced it all with him. He looked back up at her, bewildered at her anguish. She shook her head and then dropped it to her chest in an attitude of absolute dejection. What could have wounded her so in his friend's file? Dread began clawing its way towards Nicolai's heart.

"Just read it, Nicolai." With the sound of Tanya's soft voice, the dread forced its way in. He sat down without a word. Scanning the document, he quickly found cause for alarm. Sergei had been assigned, before they went to Afghanistan, to recruit Nicolai into the KGB. How long before Afghanistan had he been on their leash? The horrible possibilities crashed over him. Sergei had been the one to tell him of Anna's death. Sergei had made all the travel arrangements. Nicolai had wondered at the time how he had managed it. Sergei had identified Anna's grave. Sergei had successfully recruited him into the KGB with the promise of finding Anna's child. Sergei had found the child. After that, Sergei had faded from his life somewhat but dropped in at intervals. Nicolai had welcomed those visits, those brief reminders of a shared life and of his beloved homeland.

Everything was now in question. Was Anna even dead? Was Marta really his child? Nicolai's blood chilled at the thought of the risks he had taken, the lengths he had gone to protect that child. Yet, should he not do such things for any child? Yes! He would regret no effort for Marta. She was his daughter by right of love. One simply could not stop caring because the relationship was not of blood. And Marta was the image of Anna except for her height and strong build. She had Anna's eyes and hair. She had Nicolai's chin and strength. She was their daughter, and that added validity to that desolate grave in the Ukraine. Anna was dead. He was sure of that. Sergei had simply seen an opportunity and exploited it. What would he have done if that opportunity hadn't occurred? Did he perhaps create that opportunity? Nicolai only had Sergei's word that Anna had died in childbirth.

Nicolai shook off the spiraling horror. He had to move on from this, analyze the data not the questions. "Okay," Nicolai said aloud. "First fact: Sergei Illyvich is an enemy, not a friend."

Tears shown in Tanya's eyes as she looked up at him. He had lost his dearest friend. There was solace in the tears of another friend, one who had proven ever true. He tried to send her his gratitude through his eyes as one tear slid down her cheek, then another. Still holding the file, he moved across the room and stood next to her. She moved in closer, and he put his free arm around her.

"I'm sorry, Nicolai,"

He just nodded.

"No, I'm sorry because you must read it all."

He looked at her sharply. She lowered her eyes again. "It gets worse."

He continued to scan the material. It became clear that Sergei had been sent to break Nicolai's craft so he could be followed. The file showed a reprimand because Sergei had not been able to do so. Nicolai was alarmed by this. If anyone could break his craft, it was Sergei, and his craft had been broken. The next alarm came with Sergei's subsequent assignment: Mexico. He had been there when the Berlin Wall fell. He had been there until just before the fateful coup that was the final straw toppling the Soviet Union. Nicolai went to four alarms when he saw the code name Sergei had used there: Shatoon. Shatoon, the leader of the renegade network running drugs and protection for the Mexican drug cartels! Shatoon, the enemy who even now sought to destroy Nicolai.

There was no doubt that Peter was Shatoon's patsy, his throw-away contact man who intervened in Nicolai's operation to stop the renegades. Sergei had broken his craft and had never told Moscow. It was obvious that he'd had his own plans for that information years before he began his renegade operation. Why? What possible motive could his old friend have had to hate him so? He cast his mind back over a lifetime of friendship and stopped cold at their rivalry for Anna's attentions. Sergei had lost that rivalry, and it had almost cost them their friendship. At least Nicolai had thought it had almost cost their friendship. Obviously the friendship had begun to disintegrate and was finished by the brutal Spetsnatz training. The shock stopped Nicolai's breath for a moment. Things began to fall into place.

Sergei must have gone to the KGB after he had lost Anna. The KGB had contacted Nicolai on several occasions with offers while he had been in the army. They had probably contacted Sergei also. Both had been promising soldiers, as evidenced by their recruitment by the Spetsnatz. Knowing the KGB as he did now, Nicolai could see that they would view him as the more valuable recruit. How it must have galled Sergei to have his major value be to recruit Nicolai. Sergei had always come in second to him in everything: sports, training, subsequent missions, love affairs, and even with the KGB.

"Second fact: Sergei has hated me, viciously, all these years," Nicolai shook his head sadly.

Tanya turned to look at Nicolai, nodding slowly. "He's had years to plan, Nicolai. Judging from the target he gave Marta, we have less than twenty-four hours to stop him."

"The race! He'll do something during the race!"

Tanya stared at him.

"It's high profile, just like his intervention in our operation. He's rubbing my nose in it, can't you see? He doesn't just want to win this time. He wants to totally humiliate me. He's chosen my daughter, someone who is the image of Anna, to not only make me suffer but to let me know he's made a fool of me all these years. In other words, I didn't win."

"It makes sense," Tanya slowly enunciated as if thinking aloud. "at least from the revenge scenario, but how does it fit in with the senator's aide?"

"Perfectly," Nicolai answered grimly, "he's killing several birds with one stone. He'll use Marta to somehow discredit the war on drugs for his Mexican masters. He'll use Marta to disable or control me and my network somehow. He'll use Marta to pay me back for the loss of Anna and to bring me down from first place somehow. He'll use Marta to torture and control me." Nicolai nodded to himself and then got up to pace back and forth in the silent room.

It was all coming together, but how would Sergei do it? Nicolai's emotions were stretched to the breaking point, but he had to think. He shoved all feeling away and became purely analytical. The facts were all there, whirling around in his head. If he took them through his mental networking process, they would come together in an answer. This was his special gift and never had he needed it more. Tanya settled back on the couch, watching him pace. He felt her support like a blanket of warmth around him. Marta was the key, and the key turned in the lock at the Whaling Days race. How he knew it was beyond human language to express, but he knew it. The patterns to support that were there.

"Tanya," he turned to her abruptly, "do you think you can still keep up with Marta in a road race?"

"Yes, I've kept in shape."

"How about in disguise?"

A grin slowly spread across Tanya's face. "As the decadent capitalist Americans say, 'Piece of cake.'"

"All right. You are going to run Whaling Days with Marta. Stay close. If she wins, you come in second." He smiled at her, knowing what it had cost her all those years to hold back. She had wanted to compete for the Olympics, but the KGB had other plans for her. Nicolai still didn't know the whole story but it wasn't pretty.

She nodded, all business now, the tears dried. "I'll carry a small firearm in my running shorts. I can register that morning. I'll just get there really early."

"Good, I will station my car strategically so that I can get to her and get her out at high speed. It will be difficult with so many roads blocked for the festivities but not impossible. We will hope there is at least one FBI agent that can keep up with the two of you." Nicolai laughed out loud at the thought that there might really be no FBI agent in good enough shape to catch those two if they really let loose. He felt a sudden confidence as Tanya joined his laughter. Beyond all reason, he knew in his heart that he and Tanya and the FBI would be able to defeat Sergei and protect Marta. It was going to be all right.

"Mother needs you," Marta jumped as Peter's voice growled from behind her.

"Must you always sneak up on me, Papa?" she forced herself to ask in a sarcastically sweet tone.

Peter was not pleased. He started to raise his hand, and Marta involuntarily flinched. Peter looked around nervously at the other shoppers in the Kitsap Mall and dropped his hand. Too many witnesses, Marta concluded.

"Of course, when Mother calls, I will answer," she continued in the same sugary tone. "What does she want? I've been spending almost every waking minute with the man of her dreams. What more could she possibly need?"

"Stop your smart mouth and listen," he snapped. "You're not moving nearly fast enough with this guy. You are to compromise him, do you understand? Tonight! This is the last night before the race. He flies out tomorrow. Get to it, girl."

"Get to what?" Marta was totally confused.

"We want pictures that will embarrass him in the public eye."

"What could I possibly do to embarrass him?"

"Get him into bed, you idiot," Peter spit out in a lowered voice.

To Marta's own surprise, she burst out laughing. If this was really their plan, it was incredibly juvenile. "You can't be serious. You think that would embarrass him? Don't you read the papers? Watch the news? That wouldn't embarrass him; he'd get a medal. The man's single and from what I can glean he dates lots of women. Those women don't hesitate to sleep with him. If he wanted sex, he'd go to them. Listen to me. You go back and tell your master that I've got a much better idea. I don't sleep with the senator's aide. I marry the senator's aide. Then, whenever you want a little information from the senator or this guy's daddy, you just ask me. From what Timothy tells me of Washington parties, I'll be a walking gold mine for you people if you just don't blow it at the starting gate. Now, why don't you run along and pass that message so I can get back to my shopping? I've got a very special date tonight, and it's going to end with an engagement ring, not a one night stand."

Marta turned and left the gaping Peter to deal with his life in his own way. She was fairly confident he wouldn't shoot her in front of all these witnesses, so she decided not to worry about him. Maybe her message would bring the "big boy" out of hiding. She sincerely hoped she wouldn't find herself face to face with Uncle Nicky as the one behind this ugly farce. She was so sure it couldn't be him. He simply wasn't stupid enough to be involved in this fiasco. Who then...?

Jane came casually out of a store as Marta passed and joined her in the constantly moving mall crowd. Marta gave her a curt, quiet brief.

"What do you want me to do?" she asked as she finished.

"Continue exactly what you are doing. You handled it great. Didn't even jump too high when he made contact."

Marta chuckled, "I lambasted him for sneaking up on me. He gets so angry when I call him Papa."

"Let's forget him and shop till we drop, Girl. You are the most fun to be in an op with. I have never, ever gotten to do this much shopping before in my life and been paid for it at the same time. What a deal."

The two women enjoyed another hour of purely feminine pleasure, trying different looks, modeling for each other, and mugging for the mirror. It added to the hilarity to know that somewhere there were several people who hated shopping having to endure this to keep up the surveillance. Marta made her final purchase, a lavender flowered sun dress, and the two ladies made their way toward the VW.

"Matt." Rusty's urgent voice brought him out of deep concentration on the information they'd just received from the DEA on some possible suspects who would be interested in stopping a senator and a general from being too involved in the war on drugs. He looked up at the grim look on his colleagues face.

"I just got this on the pick-up run from the drop box." Rusty held a note out to him. "It's okay. I've had it dusted for prints. Luckily the guy who picked it up didn't recognize the handwriting and got nervous. He treated it as evidence from the get-go."

"Good thinking," Matt agreed as he took the offending item. He read with growing alarm. It was a warning to watch the Whaling Days race carefully. "What do you make of this?"

"One, someone knows our movements well enough to know where the drop box is. Two, they know we've got people in the race tomorrow. Three, this is either a set-up or a challenge."

"I don't agree with number three," Matt surprised himself by blurting out.

"What?"

"There could be another possibility. Someone could be warning us," Matt theorized out loud.

"Who, for crying out loud? We've got enough players in this game already without another faction coming in trying to warn us about what some other faction is doing."

"I don't think we've got a new player here. Don't ask me why, but I think this is from Marta's Uncle Nicky."

"Nicolai Androvich Gorgonov? Why would he warn us? I thought he was the fish we were after?"

"Rusty, it's just a thought. Maybe it's a stupid thought, but it's a thought. Don't rule it out completely. We could confirm, though," Matt suggested tentatively, somehow not liking the idea. "Has anyone called the phone number Marta's Uncle Nicky gave her for emergencies?"

"Got an answering machine. Left a number, got no answer. Traced it to the tavern you are currently working in. It led us in a circle. Which brings me to my fourth point. Do you know just how fast Marta is? Do you think a couple of us can stay close to her?"

"Ask our target. He's seen her run."

"Yeah, but not flat out. She's not going to hold back tomorrow. She challenged Parsons to a race, and, judging from the look in her eyes, if she loses, she's going to make him break a record. Know what I mean?" Matt grinned. He hoped she could run that guy into the ground for all the years he and his buddies had leered at her and made her feel like a freak. Then he asked forgiveness for his lack of charity and got back to the problem at hand.

"I've run with her. I think Feldman and I can keep up with her on a short race. Feldman's probably the only one who could go the distance in a longer run. She's a marathoner, and most of us don't have the time to keep up that kind of training."

"We'll ask for Feldman to stay close. The military said they'd give us some marines on this. Tell them we'll spread it around the barracks that we think they can't keep up with our lady. That should be sufficient incentive to keep them neck and neck." Rusty was obviously enjoying this. Matt was not so sure he was. They'd raced back to the apartment almost every morning, and she'd about run him into the ground a couple of times.

"We've got plenty of cover, then. Will the marines be armed?"

"Yes, but they're instructed to carry small arms, concealed. They are to follow your lead, Matt. Each one has been given a picture of you, Marta, and Parsons. They've also been given the best descriptions we have of Nicolai Androvich Gorgonov and a still from our video tapes of that creep Peter."

"I'll have a clip-on two-way radio with earphones that looks like a smart phone. I'll have to use a flat side-arm, so my issue piece isn't going to cut it, Rusty. I'm using my .25 caliber Colt Pocket Automatic Pistol."

"I didn't hear that," Rusty grinned. "It'd be like the suits to gig you for not sticking a monstrous piece in your shorts, man. I mean, with the radio and the piece, you're going to be lucky to keep your pants up as it is."

"That's all I need, to get caught with my pants down," Matt chuckled. "Oh, well, my shirt hangs over the waistband. That'll help some."

"Bureaucrats. . . gotta love 'em. Let's us working stiffs get back out on the scene and catch the bad guys," Rusty clapped Matt on the shoulder, laughing.

"I'll clean up here and meet you in the lobby. Where'd we leave the truck?"

"Down at the supermarket. I'm going to pick up some stuff there for the place. Why don't you meet me by the ice cream stand? Go through that construction site back up the hill."

Matt groaned.

"Ah, the walk will be good conditioning for the big race tomorrow."

"Yeah, right, the ice cream will be better conditioning," Matt laughed as he closed the file he'd been working and signed off the computer. Rusty, already half way out the door, turned and gave him the thumbs up sign. Matt wasn't sure if it was for the race or the ice cream.

CHAPTER FIFTEEN

Marta's alarm brought her bolt upright Saturday morning. She must have dozed off sometime in the early morning, but she couldn't remember getting any sleep. She and Timothy had gone to a community theater performance for their special "last night" date and had stayed out late to make things look good. All she'd wanted when she finally got home was sleep.

She heard movement in the next apartment and knew that at least one of them was up, probably Matt. Marta pulled her upper body into a straight- backed stretch and hopped out of bed to complete her stretching routine.

This might be her last chance at winning a race, and she was going for it. This might be her last chance at anything. Death did not hold the horror for her it had before she accepted Jesus. Was it just a little over a week ago? It seemed a lifetime ago. No, death didn't scare her, but dying without ever having lived did scare her. She wanted to live and love and have children and be normal for a little while. She sent up a prayer, letting her preferences be known but leaving it all in God's hands. Then she lost herself in preparation for a race.

Matt, too, had slept little the night before. He heard Marta moving around and knew she was up. Jane came in and started breakfast.

"You want anything, Matt?"

"I don't usually eat before a race, but I better have something light. It could be a very long time before we have time to eat again.

"Pessimist," Rusty teased as he entered the kitchen. "It won't take you that long to finish the race, and I've heard there are major food booths at this festival. I'm going to be a regular pig."

Matt's tension dissipated under Rusty's good natured teasing. He prayed that Marta would have peace as well.

"Tanya, are you ready?" Nicolai asked tensely and turned to see a dark-haired, brown-eyed, deeply-tanned woman come through the door in pink running shorts with a matching top. "Ah, I see you are. The disguise is good."

"Yes, as long as this tan from a bottle doesn't streak when you sweat," Tanya laughed, sounding a little nervous. Nicolai couldn't blame her. They were all very exposed, he and Tanya and Marta. There was nothing he could do about it, though. They had passed the point of no return when he had activated Marta.

"You know where I will be with the car in case anything happens. Signal me with this if we need to get wheels to Marta quickly." He held up a small black case with a tiny antenna which Tanya clipped to the band of her shorts and covered with her top. "I'll be monitoring you, so stay as close as you can to Marta. You may be the only two women in the front of the pack, so there's no way to be unobtrusive about this. Just stick with her."

"It will be my pleasure, Nicolai. I've always wanted to win a mother-daughter race with Marta." She gave him a teasing grin. He shook his head at her attempt to lighten things up. Then he took three deep breaths. Today he could lose everything, Marta, Tanya, and his own life. For what? To protect whom? He'd risked Marta to stop these monsters. Why couldn't he have left it to the FBI, given them anonymous tips or something? No, the great Nicolai Androvich Gorgonov had gotten cocky and decided he could have his daughter and save the world, too. Well, too late now. He took another deep breath. The tender look in Tanya's eyes was almost his undoing. He had never before realized how much Tanya viewed Marta as her daughter, loved her as she would have her own child if she had been able to have one. She was risking it all too.

He reached out and took her hand in his. "God be with you, today, my friend," Where had that come from, he wondered. Yet he had spoken it with his own lips.

"And with you, Nicolai," she breathed softly as she reached up and brushed a butterfly kiss on his cheek. Then she disengaged her hand from his, almost as if it took an act of supreme will, and left the apartment.

Nicolai waited until he was sure she was clear of the area. Then he left to clear his path to his vantage point on a hill above the street on which the racers would pass later that morning.

The staging area for the race was exciting. Marta had always loved the crowding at the starting line after all the runners had their numbers pinned on and were vying for a good starting position. It was all good will and comradery. Best of all, she could stand right next to Matt, and no one would care.

Timothy spotted her right away. His buddies stood with mouths gaping and eyes wide as he casually walked over and kissed her in front of everyone. She'd smiled and received it but wanted to slap him for using her to show off to his friends. Matt's face was an expressionless mask when she glanced up at him after Timothy's public embrace. How could she ever let him know that every caress from Timothy only made her long for him all the more?

Today had all the earmarks of a crisis. Marta could feel it in the air. She felt sure that whatever was going to happen would happen today. It had to. Timothy was flying out for DC tonight. What would happen with Matt after all this was over?

Tension rippled through the crowd of racers, and the starting signal sounded. A surge of humanity moved into the tunnel of cheering on-lookers, and Marta lost all thought but of running to win. The faster runners started jockeying for position to break out of the crowd and open up a lead. Marta saw an opening and went for it. She could feel Matt moving beside her but lost all sense of Timothy's presence. They ran neck and neck into a clear space and kicked into stride, eating up the pavement before them.

They made the first turn, off the main street of Silverdale, and started up hill. Marta could sense some of the runners slipping back, but she kept her pace relentlessly. She could hear Matt breathing next to her but knew he was okay with the pace. She pressed on, conquering the hill. She could feel her heart and lungs pumping in an exquisite rhythm. All was right with her world.

They crested the hill and hit the next relatively flat stretch. Marta lengthened her stride, pulling everything she could get from each footfall. Matt was right there, steady, strong. They were together, running as one. She loved him fiercely and dared to hope.

Suddenly, without warning, a car screeched to a halt beside her, strong arms grabbed her, and she was trapped inside a speeding vehicle with runners scattering to get out of the way.

Matt watched in horror as two men pulled Marta into their car. It was a classic KGB snatch. Why hadn't he seen this as a possibility? Why hadn't he taken precautions? He was helpless, no car near enough for a chase. They'd all pulled back, but he knew the FBI would be following quickly. He shouted a description of the car into his radio even as he realized with horror that he, personally, could not follow. He could not be the one to protect her; he would have to trust that to others. Still he ran down the road after the car. A car pulled up next to him, and the door was thrown open. He didn't stop to question. He just got in, and it careened into high gear after the fleeing vehicle. His only thought was to get to Marta. He continued giving directions to the other chase vehicles. They were headed north. They'd passed through the Highway 3 intersection toward Poulsbo before he looked at the driver.

Matt knew with certainty it was Nicolai Androvich Gorgonov who was driving with the intensity of an Indy 500 driver and about as well. Matt simply accepted that Gorgonov was as intent on getting to Marta as he was. For the moment, they were on the same side. Matt welcomed his skill. If anyone could stick to a KGB escape car, this man could. Matt continued radioing in directions to the other chase cars. He monitored the radio traffic enough to know they were having great difficulty catching up. They had to follow the rules. He and Gorgonov didn't. Matt knew that even if it cost him his badge, he'd catch up to her. His only worry was harming an innocent bystander. From the way Gorgonov handled the car, Matt didn't think that would happen. He thought he'd make the stipulation anyway.

"Just don't kill any innocent bystanders, okay?"

Gorgonov grunted and kept his eyes resolutely on the speeding car in front of them. They left Highway 3 and headed onto side roads where there was less traffic.

They turned left speeding through an intersection guarded by huge wooden carvings of trolls. Its charm was lost on the hunted and the prey. Gorgonov was relentless. It appeared this was as personal to him as it was to Matt. What was the connection? He called another change in direction to the other chase car.

"It looks like they're headed to Hansville. They'll have full access to the deep water from there and plenty of available boats. Better alert the Coast Guard."

"Have them look for a large freighter, heading back out to open ocean through the Hood Canal. Remind them that this is a hostage situation," Gorgonov growled without taking his eyes from the car holding Marta. It was the first words he'd spoken, his deep bass without a hint of accent.

Matt passed the information on without question. So far, everyone had been intent on the chase and hadn't asked about his own situation. They probably each assumed he was in the other car. Good. He didn't have time to explain.

They sped through Hansville and headed back south on the other side of the Kitsap peninsula. It was obvious they had a very specific destination in mind. They finally made the turn onto Hood Canal Drive Northeast and then into the small residential area of Driftwood Key. He called in their position and then concentrated on keeping the car in sight as it turned into the private marina.

The car in front squealed to a stop, and the people bailed out. Marta was hauled from the back seat, a gun at her head. Gorgonov and Matt braked to a squealing stop behind them. They ran along the dock and halted as one when the man holding Marta made a threatening gesture toward her with the gun.

"Nicolai," rasped the small, blond man, "stay back or you can watch her die right here! I'd warn you not to follow, but the entrance to this marina will be high and dry almost as soon as my boat is through it. You see, Nicolai, you are not the master you thought you were."

"Sergei, stop this madness. It's not too late!"

"It was too late when you killed my Anna!"

"No, Sergei. Don't take Marta, please," he begged.

Evil laughter was the only answer as the man dragged Marta on to a well-equipped fishing boat, its motor already throbbing. The minute they were on board, the boat headed for the mouth of the marina. Already the water allowing passage into and out of the small marina was receding. Matt's heart sank as the boat headed out into open water.

"Hey, you." Matt looked around to see a well-muscled, gray-haired man sticking his head up from the cabin of the fishing boat next to them. "I can still get this boat out of here in time. Go back up the road and turn left onto the spit. There's a private dock there. Meet me at the end of it. You're the good guys, right?" the man paused to question.

Matt discreetly flashed his badge.

"Good. Take off in your car. They'll think you're gone. I'll just casually pull out like I'm going fishing, didn't see or hear anything," he grinned, pointing to his hearing aids. "Move it. My exit's closing."

Matt grabbed Gorgonov's shoulder, bringing him out of a horrified trance. "I'll drive. Get in. We've got a reprieve." Matt barked as the fishing boat next to him started its seemingly leisurely way toward the rapidly receding water at the mouth of the marina. Gorgonov sprang to life and jumped into the passenger seat as Matt put the still running car into gear. Matt spotted the road onto the spit and went to the very end. There was indeed a small private dock. Matt prayed he and Gorgonov would not get shot for trespassing.

"Come on, Gorgonov. Our ride's here."

"How did you manage this?" a bewildered Gorgonov growled.

"As we say in America, 'Don't look a gift horse in the mouth.' Just hurry." Matt killed the engine, and they jumped out, running toward the waiting boat. The captain, as Matt mentally referred to their benefactor, motioned them on board.

"Stay down." The captain yelled. "I've got some other clothes that might fit you in the cabin. They're just pulling around Foulweather Bluff, but they might look back. I want 'em to think I'm picking up my fishing buddies. That sourpuss who owns the boat might have been around here enough to have seen me do that a few times. Knows I wear hearing aids, too. Made a smart aleck remark to me one day, and I pretended not to hear so I wouldn't have to punch him in the nose."

"We'll take it from here, Sir." Matt indicated the dock, trying to encourage the man to leave his boat in their hands.

"You want to catch that boat and save that girl, or you want to argue about who's gonna drive, Son?"

Gorgonov apparently recovered from his shock, "Ignore him and drive. That's my daughter they've got."

The man didn't wait to answer. He expertly maneuvered the boat away from the dock and headed to open water.

"Name's Bob, by the way," the captain tossed over his shoulder. "I know these waters and can outmaneuver that jerk any time. He's been a real pain around here. Bought a lot just for the marina space. Real unfriendly and ignores all common courtesy. Kind of happy to know he's gonna get his when we catch him. Got binoculars under the seat back there. You're free to use them. They just rounded the bluff, so I'll pull around, casual like, and see if I can catch sight of them while you're below."

They ducked into the cabin. As they changed clothes, Matt gave the older man a perplexed look. "You said they had your daughter?"

In response, Matt received a gentle smile, filled with great sadness.

Matt felt his eyes sting with unshed tears. "They took your daughter from you, and you followed any way you could."

Nicolai nodded in assent. "I had to be successful, you see, to gain some control over my whereabouts," he explained. "I had to gain their confidence to find my little girl. It's no excuse, I know, for damaging others, but I did as little damage as I could. I refused to suck the life out of people for a little useless information. I bought taverns and taught my people to listen. Most people who gave us information didn't even know they were doing it. I never took unnecessary risks. I had to stay by my little one." Nicolai turned away and headed up to the deck. Matt followed.

"Thanks, Bob. By the way, I'm Matt, and this is Nick. Can you steer this thing in a crouch when we get close to these guys? They are definitely armed and dangerous. I'm already in enough trouble for taking the boat. I'd prefer not to have to explain injuries to a civilian."

"We get close; I go down. You can either take the wheel or call out directions. I spotted them up ahead there," he gestured with his head rather than pointing, and Matt wondered about the guy's background. He seemed to be savvy about discreet surveillance techniques.

"What you gonna do when we catch 'em?" Bob asked.

"You heard their threats. It all depends on where my daughter is and whether we can get aboard the other boat before they hurt her." Nicolai answered quietly.

"Those binoculars will come in very handy in planning the next stage, don't you think, Matt?"

Matt knew an order when he heard one. He left and found the binoculars, briefly noting the tools and extra rope neatly stored under the seat. They were gaining on the speeding boat ahead of them. Matt used the binoculars in a sweep, as if looking at the scenery. He described the position of everyone on the other boat but pointed towards the landscape. Nicolai took the glasses from him, beginning the same process.

Matt's radio crackled to life, reminding him of its presence. He sat up against the cabin to hide his activity from the boat ahead and answered.

"Matt, where are you?" Frank's voice was laced with tension. He'd thrown radio procedure out the window, too. Perhaps there was hope for Matt's career yet.

"On a private boat headed to the northbound shipping lanes of the Puget Sound, following the suspects."

"You're on a private boat, not with the Coast Guard?"

"Affirmative."

"Coast Guard has you on radar and is on the way. They had a cutter keeping an eye on a Mexican freighter. You and the suspects are headed for it. We'll follow with back-up as soon as the Coast Guard picks us up. Stay well behind until back-up arrives. This became a Coast Guard operation as soon as it got wet. You read me, ol' man?"

Matt rubbed the radio mouthpiece over the back of the captain's chair. "Sorry, I'm having some interference. Couldn't catch last transmission. We are heading into northbound shipping lanes and, I assume, into open ocean. Suspects are apparently meeting up with a larger ship. We will attempt to apprehend before they make contact with it." He rubbed the radio mouthpiece against the railing of the boat, creating a horrible noise. Then he turned it off. He had told Frank his intentions. He was going to get Marta out, no matter what the orders were.

"There it is," Matt called as he spotted the freighter. It was a container ship. It was high in the water, apparently carrying a light load. He'd never realized how big those freighters were until he began approaching one in a small boat.

The other boat pulled up beside the freighter. Matt watched helplessly as a great loading door was opened at the water line and Marta was forced into the freighters depths. The other boat was left abandoned to drift, the wake of the freighter momentarily holding it to the side.

"Lord, God, how are we going to get up that?" Matt didn't realize he was praying aloud as he looked up the massive side of the freighter. How could anyone get on it uninvited?

"Get up that?" Bob interjected, "Getting close to it with that powerful bow and stern wake will be a trick." As if to demonstrate, the empty boat drifted into just the wrong place and was sucked under. Matt drew in a sharp breath.

"Yes, my friend," Gorgonov's growl came from beside him. "A miracle is needed. You pray. I will think. I think better when I'm fishing. Bob, do you have gear for us?"

Matt looked at him in surprise. Of course, it was the perfect cover. Matt looked around and saw a number of other small fishing boats bobbing in the Puget Sound, giving the shipping lanes wide birth. Bob looked pinched and tense as he broke out the fishing gear, and they all chose a position, close enough to hear each other. All three began to look around the boat for whatever tools might be useful.

"I have this," Bob said, setting his pole aside and pulling a block and tackle with a steel hook on the end from a storage space under his seat. It looked strong. "It's from my Alaska fishing days for catching deep water fish. Don't know why I keep it.

Memories, I guess. That gear will hold the weight of a halibut or other large fish. We could pull the rope out of the block pulleys so we have a free line for the hook as a grappler. With enough rope, maybe we could get the hook up there."

They all looked at the huge freighter. Yes, a miracle was needed. Matt went back and got the length of rope he'd noticed earlier. Bob joined the two sections of rope with the expertise of long years at sea. It had to be enough.

"Lord," Matt spoke urgently and from the heart, "we can't do this ourselves. We need You to guide Bob next to the freighter and then get him safely away. The rope may not be long enough. Even if we have the strength to throw it that high, we may not have the strength to climb it. If by a miracle, you allow us to hook the deck railing; our enemies could be alerted by it and be waiting for us. Assuming we can make the climb, we won't know until we're over the railing if we're simply giving ourselves over to the enemy. Lord, we have no other option. We're going to trust You and go for it. In our weakness, show Your strength."

Bob and Gorgonov stared at him open-mouthed. "Well, you said I was to pray. Have you been thinking?"

"Yes, I have, and we are going to have to map out strategy here. The engine noise will drown any attempts at conversation. Bob, can you go to the lowest point on the railing?" Gorgonov pointed to the railing adjacent to the container section of the ship.

"That should be a good place for you guys," Bob explained. "Looks like there's still enough cargo to hide your movements. Not much crew on these container ships, usually about nine. With the two we saw going on, no more than eleven with a pilot who could be a real ally."

"Or another hostage," Matt thought out loud.

"This is as good as it gets," Gorgonov firmly closed the discussion. "We'll throw for the deck railing at the lowest point. I will try first until my arm tires. Then, Matt, you will do the same. We'll keep doing that until we either die or we get on board.

Get into the front passenger seat and sit. Bob will keep the boat steady from a seated position. I don't wish to decapitate anyone. I will go first. If I die, I charge you to save my daughter. You will have warning. Use it well."

"Bob, can you maintain control of the boat from a position close enough to rescue us in case we fall?"

Bob nodded, adjusting the controls with the air of a seasoned sailor.

"If we're fired on, leave immediately. Otherwise, when we are aboard, go home with our thanks."

Gorgonov turned back to Matt, picking up a life preserver with hooked belts dangling on the ends.

"We'll use these to hook to the line. Does not your Bible say that all things are possible with God? So, we will go with God."

Matt nodded assent and added, "Before we do this, I just thought of something else. It's an old rock climber's trick we can use to rest on the way up when we need to." Matt picked up an extra length of rope at the back of the boat and, with Bob's permission, cut it into two equal lengths. "You knot the rope like this." He then demonstrated the climber's technique of using one knot to pull one foot up while resting the other foot in a second knot. Next he handed Nicolai one length of rope.

Nicolai practiced the knots quickly while Bob returned to the controls, circling back toward the stern of the huge ship. Expertly maneuvering the boat at just the right point in the wake, he pulled the boat into the shadow of the hull midpoint between the superstructure and the stern.

Nicolai steadied himself as well as he could and began circling the rope, the barbed hook swinging a larger and larger arc in the absolute control of Gorgonov's massive arms. The circling went faster and suddenly, with a move of incredible grace and power, Gorgonov launched it toward the deck railing. It hit the rail with a clang and splashed into the water. They waited for gun fire. There was none.

"Thank you, Lord, for the first miracle. It looks like no one saw it hit." Matt said softly as Gorgonov began the circling process again. Again came the launch, the clang, the splash, the wait, and the prayer of thanks.

They had each taken several turns; Matt's attempts clumsy and nowhere close to the mark. Again Gorgonov stepped into position. He had been studying Matt's attempts. He began circling with a slightly different motion. The radius of his circle was smaller. He gained greater speed with the smaller circle launched with a full body thrust, rocking the boat as he did so. He risked capsizing to get greater lift. The hook went over the railing. Gorgonov pulled it back until it hit something and lodged. He yanked several times, hard, risking capsizing again. He looked at Matt and laid his hand on his shoulder before he tied his knots and began his assent. Matt felt as if he were receiving a father's blessing.

Once he was a few feet up, Nicolai nodded to him and Matt tied his knots and began his own assent. He didn't look down. He kept his eyes resolutely above as they worked their way slowly up the side. Gorgonov was setting a killer pace. Matt wondered how old the guy was. He was moving up the side like a twenty-year-old world class rock climber.

"Lord, please help me to keep up and not just for pride's sake. Marta's life may well depend on how fast we get there, but then You know more about that than I do."

Matt's arms felt as if they were giving out and his legs had turned to rubber before Nicolai stopped for the first rest. He sucked air into his lungs, praying strength into his failing muscles. He hoped Frank would get a helicopter there soon as a distraction when he and Nicolai had to scramble over the deck railing. Frank would think of something like that.

Matt prayed for peace and courage for Marta. At least she didn't have to face this alone. She had the King of the universe with her.

Gorgonov started climbing again and all thought, all prayer, all effort went into getting one hand over the other. Sure enough, just as Gorgonov reached the deck railing, Matt heard the sound of a chopper. "Bless you, Frank," he muttered through clenched teeth as he made the last hard climb, then rested as Gorgonov made his silent way over the railing. Matt heard shouts and the sound of running, but they were not close by. Gorgonov's body didn't fly over the side and Matt heard no gunfire, so he took courage and launched himself over the railing. He pulled his Colt Pocket Automatic as soon as he stabilized on the deck. Gorgonov was also armed with a Designer Walther 9MM and was hiding behind a looming stack of containers. Matt joined him.

The sounds of yelling and running were on the other side of the deck. Obviously, Frank had seen them climbing and ordered in a distraction to buy them time to find Marta.

"Sounds like the cavalry has arrived," Nicolai yelled above the engine noise. "We must make our way forward to the superstructure. My guess is she'll be in one of the crew cabins."

Matt acknowledged with a nod and moved forward until they found a door. He covered Nicolai as he pulled it open, breathing a sigh of relief that it was neither locked nor guarded. They made their way into the narrow corridor listening for the slightest sound to indicate the location of Marta Alexander.

CHAPTER SIXTEEN

Marta stared into the cold, gray eyes of a predator. Her captor was a small man, but his size was immaterial. The threat he posed was in his merciless stare. He was studying her as if she were a specimen he was about to dissect. Horror shivered through her as she prayed desperate, wordless prayers.

"You are very like her, you know," the cold, almost metallic voice brought Marta up sharp. She gave him a blank stare but said nothing. He laughed a dry, mirthless choking laugh, almost like a machine expelling air.

"Your mother, of course," he answered her unasked question. She refused to be sucked in. This was a classic KGB interrogation technique. Bring up a minute piece of true information or some general statement that would seem to the victim that you knew everything about them when you knew next to nothing. Of course she would be very like her mother, most people are like their parents, and how would Marta know if she weren't?

"She was very beautiful, just as you are," he leered, bringing his face into hers. The bonds that tied her to a chair kept her from pulling away from him as her every instinct screamed to do.

He reached out a bony finger and ran the nail down her face, leaving a scratch and a sting in its path. "Yes, she was very beautiful, as you are, but then your father got hold of her. Now, she's dead. Yes, you came, and she went. Poof." He shook his head in wonder as if the thought simply amazed him. He stared into her eyes, seeming to demand a response. She gave him none. "Well," he said crisply, moving back from her in a business-like manner, evidently closing one piece of business and heading into the next item on the agenda, "enough of that. This is now. Your mother has been gone many years, and you are a grown woman, one who will be very valuable to me. Alive you are valuable, so you needn't worry I will kill you. You see, your father is interfering in my business. My associates and I are very upset with him. He must be brought under control." The man turned and smiled a slow, ugly smile. "You, my dear, are the perfect control on your father's behavior."

"Humph," Marta couldn't withhold a sarcastic grunt. Her father had given her over to the State to do with her what they wanted. What would he care what happened to her?

"Ah, I see you do not believe me. How precious. You think your father does not care about you. You are very wrong, you know. He has risked everything and played a very dangerous game just to be near you. He played the role of master spy, while all he was really doing was taking care of his little girl. He never even sent Moscow any real information. He gathered little bits and pieces and made up the rest. It's amazing how true his guesses were. I watched. I know he did not use traditional methods. Yet, he was almost always right. Think of the risks he took, My Dear, to be near you yet retain what little honor he thought he had. But he relinquished all honor when he killed your mother with his lust, the foul pig." Rage colored the gray face with red for a moment. Then he seemed to regain control of himself.

It suddenly occurred to Marta that, by some miracle, someone might be looking for her. There had been a boat behind them all the way to the freighter. How they'd board or who they were she didn't know, but she knew in her heart that if Matt could find a way to get to her he would. The sound of her voice might bring help to her faster.

"What does all this have to do with me? I don't even know my real name. I never knew my mother or my father."

"You are wrong, My Dear. You do know your father."

Marta looked at him long and hard. A horrible thought occurred to her.

"You don't mean Peter was really my father?"

That brought a real laugh from her captor. "No, no, no. Wrong guess, My Dear. What other man was ever hovering near, interfering in all sorts of matters that were really none of his business? Who did Tanya call when she needed someone to control Peter? Eh? Was there no protector in your youth?"

"Uncle Nicky," she breathed. The world began to recede before her eyes. She couldn't faint. She must show no weakness. This one before her was one of the mad dogs Uncle Nicky had talked about. Uncle Nicky was her father. It all made perfect sense. And she had betrayed him. That realization must have shown on her face, for her captor beamed triumph from every pore. She wanted to spit in his face but knew it would only incite him while accomplishing nothing.

"Yes, your beloved Uncle Nicky is really your father. You were not the only one he took risks for, though. He has a network all his own. He has grand ideas of patriotism, you see. He plans to save our country, to save the world!" Her tormentor laughed at his own joke, hugely enjoying the role of buffoon into which he cast her father.

Marta found the thought rather comforting in spite of everything. Her father had cared enough to find her and protect her as well as he could.

"No, our hero couldn't stop there, he had to go and build his little network of 'patriots,'" he spit out the last word in contempt, "to interfere with certain of my business dealings. He got so bold as to plant one of his operatives in my organization." Again, barely controlled rage was apparent. "That was the person you were supposed to meet that day in Seattle, but my operative intervened. Yes, dear Peter works for me now. He's not very smart, but he does have his uses. For one, he got to you before your daddy's friend could. I would love to have seen Nicolai's face when you walked off that ferry with Peter."

"What purpose can you possibly have for all this? You're crazy!" Marta realized her strategic error immediately. This guy really was crazy, and he didn't like being called that. He proved it with a sharp blow across her face. The world became a red haze for just a moment. Then her vision cleared, and she looked into the eyes of hatred.

"My purpose is to make Nicolai hurt as much as he hurt me by killing Anna! And you, you murdering little brat, will be the implement of torture I use to make that purpose a reality." Rage receded and cunning replaced it. "You will also be a great asset to my associates and me since you and Mr. Parsons made such a photogenic couple. You've been seen together everywhere. You went to an elegant fund raiser with him in your shiny pink gown, making the front page of a number of newspapers and the tabloid news. Everyone is wondering who Timothy Parsons, one of Washington DC's most eligible bachelors, is courting so intensely. Could it be? Why yes, it's the same woman who will now be photographed gracing the arm of one of Mexico's most notorious drug lords. Won't Mr. Parson's boss be embarrassed? Won't Dear Papa be worried? Perhaps Dear Papa will think you've come over to our side. What does he call us? Mad dogs, isn't it?"

The syrupy sweet tones made her nauseous as the truth sank in. If someone didn't get her off this boat before it hit Mexican coast, this mad man could actually succeed in his plan. Timothy, his father, and the senator would all be rendered powerless. Their program to continue fierce intervention in Mexican drug production and export would be gutted, killed by innuendo. Marta felt the deepest despair she'd ever known. She would rather die than live as this man's pawn. Her heart cried out, the words escaped, "Oh Lord, don't let my enemies triumph over me!"

He slapped her again, and the world whirled in a red haze.

Matt followed Nicolai, both guns at the ready. They searched the first deck, cautiously opened doors, until sounds through the stairwell to the second deck riveted them to the spot. A man's cold, merciless voice carried clearly in the silence. Matt recognized the voice of Marta's kidnapper and Timothy Parson's name. He waited for Nicolai to signal him, deferring to his obviously superior knowledge of the situation.

Nicolai had just turned to signal Matt, when they both heard Marta's clear voice, "Oh, Lord, don't let my enemies triumph over me." It galvanized them into action, and they moved in controlled stealth up the stairwell. There was only one door, right at the top, from which the voices could have come that clearly. A brief reconnaissance from the top of the stairs, and they were across. Matt signaled to Nicolai, and then pointed to the door. Nicolai nodded, grim determination on his face. Matt knew without words that Nicolai would go in first to draw any fire. Matt was to make sure that Marta got out of there safely no matter what. They both understood. One of them had to remain healthy to get her out; the other had to be willing to sacrifice himself. Nicolai chose himself to do the sacrificing and Matt had to accept that because it made the best sense for Marta. Matt could help her afterwards. Nicolai couldn't.

Her tormentor laughed, "There is no one out there to hear your prayer, Pretty One. You are mine. I am the only power there is for you now, Little...."

He broke off at a sharp sound at the door, which suddenly crashed inward. He raised his gun to fire, but Marta spun herself, chair and all, into him. The shot went wild. She could feel the vermin beneath her trying to wiggle free, and she pounded her chair into him with her full body weight. It was awkward but effective if the sounds coming from him were any measure. She looked up into the golden warmth of Matt's eyes. He gave her a business-like nod, indicating he had things under control so she could stop bouncing on the guy. She rolled away to give Matt a clear shot should he need one.

"Get her off me," screamed the downed man. "You fools, where have you...."

"FBI," Matt flashed a badge with the hand not holding his Colt. "Drop the gun and lie face down, spread eagle."

A sound from near the door caught Marta's attention as Matt gave the man his rights. She wiggled over to find Uncle Nicky. . .her father...holding his right shoulder. It was bleeding. She tried to free herself from the remaining pieces of the chair, but her hands were still securely fastened to something.

She looked at her father. His eyes were closed. He was bleeding, and she was helpless. She moved closer and heard him groan.

"Uncle Nicky, are you okay?" she queried softly in a language she hadn't used in many years.

His eyes opened slowly, and they simply looked at each other, father and daughter. "Just once, call me Papa," he whispered softly and passed out.

The sounds of running feet came from the passageway and Marta tensed, then relaxed. Rusty came through the door, gun first and all business. He covered Nicolai as he surveyed the scene. Jane followed in the same manner. She kept her revolver at the ready as she spoke into a small radio.

"We have the second deck secured. Looks like two bad guys down, one bleeding." Rusty bent down and began applying pressure to Nicolai's wounds.

"There's only one bad guy here," Matt said softly. "The one who's bleeding is a father trying to protect his daughter." Matt's eyes met Marta's, and she sent gratitude toward him with all her heart. "Someone, please untie the lady and handcuff this guy."

Jane handcuffed Sergei and then proceeded to untie Marta. Marta cautiously leaned around Rusty to check for a pulse in her father's throat. Thank the Lord there was a pulse, a bit fluttery but there.

"Here," Jane's voice brought Marta's head around. Jane handed her a white handkerchief to press against the bleeding shoulder. "You know where to apply pressure?"

Marta nodded.

"Take over for Rusty, then."

Marta took Rusty's place and pressed the handkerchief against her papa's shoulder. He would live. He had to live. She had so much to say, so many questions. Who was Anna? Was she really like her mother? Who was this terrible man, and why did he want to hurt Nicolai? Did he really risk everything just to be near her? Could they be together now?

Matt's boss, Frank, came in, followed by a couple of coast guard guys with a stretcher. Marta watched him take charge without a word. Matt seemed to come down from alert, as did everyone else. The coast guard paramedic gently lifted her hand away from her father's shoulder.

"We'll take care of him now, Ma'am."

"I want to be with him." She turned to Frank who'd been directing the disposition of their prisoner "Can I go with my father, please? He's hurt."

He turned to her, looking surprised. He turned back to Matt.

"Nicolai Androvich Gorgonov is her natural father. He told me on the way out. My radio was picking up interference so I couldn't report that."

"Yeah, we didn't get anything but static during your last report and then dead air."

Some kind of unspoken communication passed between the two men, but Marta was too weary to care what it all meant. They seemed to think there was something more important in the universe than her being with her new papa. What fools, why didn't they answer her?

Frank finally turned back to her. "You may meet them at the hospital as long as there is an agent with you. They'll evacuate him on the Coast Guard helicopter, and there's no room, much less time to pull you up, too. Even at the hospital, he is going to be under guard. You understand that?"

She nodded.

"I'd like to go with her," Matt volunteered.

"Fine, but I want another agent with you. I don't want any questions about what happened today. It certainly looked like you were aiding and abetting out there. The military's pretty angry."

"Ah, the military's always angry."

"Get out of here before you get us both fired. Jane, you go with them."

"We've got to go, Sir," one of the paramedics said crisply. "This guy's losing' blood. We've got to get him on the chopper, now!"

"Go." Frank moved everyone out of their way. "The rest of us will follow on the cutter." Matt took Marta's elbow, and they hurried into the passageway and up the stairs. Frank and Rusty followed with the prisoner sandwiched between them. Marta heard shouts and gunshots as she and Matt ran toward the chopper behind Jane. The man who had kidnapped her was throwing himself, still handcuffed, over the railing. She didn't stop to sort that out. Nicolai was of main importance just then. She watched as the expert Coast Guard rescue team loaded him into a stretcher attached to the hovering helicopter. Nicolai was still unconscious with a tube running into his arm. She breathed a prayer of hope as she watched him being pulled slowly up to the waiting chopper.

CHAPTER SEVENTEEN

Matt stayed by Marta throughout the ordeal of getting Nicolai into the hospital. He continued by her side as they waited to hear about his condition. Jane was soon relieved as guard and joined them in the waiting room. Rusty and Frank called in periodically from the office to get updates. Finally the doctor came out briefly to tell them that Nicolai, although he had lost a great deal of blood, would recover.

"He's being moved into intensive care right now. Only one of you may go in to see him and just for a second," the doctor said sternly.

Marta thanked him, and Matt saw tears in her eyes. She looked so tired and fragile, and he ached to hold and protect her. Now was not the time to impose his feelings on her.

Marta turned to Jane, "May I be the one to go in?"

"You go in, dear," Jane affirmed. "We will watch like a hawk to make sure you don't run off with him." Jane's humor was rewarded with a small, tight smile from Marta.

They made their way to intensive care. Jane cleared it with the guard and the nurse for Marta to go in. Matt watched through the glass as she bent over the unconscious old warhorse and kissed him tenderly on the forehead. She laid a hand on his head, and Matt knew she was praying. He joined her and knew Jane was praying as well.

When she came out, she came straight toward Matt, and he opened his arms. She walked into them, and he held her close, wrapping her in his love for a few seconds. She was reeling with exhaustion.

"Let's get you home, Marta," Matt said gently, his cheek pressed to her hair. "You're about to fall asleep on your feet."

She nodded.

"Does anybody have a car?" the ever-practical Jane queried. Matt's mind went blank. The Coast Guard had dropped them off and left. He had no clue where to get a car.

"Sorry," Jane continued ruefully, "I should have thought of that hours ago, but I was so busy praying."

Everyone gave a little chuckle.

"Tell you what, I'll call Rusty and see if he can pick us up. In the meantime, we could eat something. I have no idea how long it's been since any of us have eaten."

"Too long," Matt said, suddenly realizing he was ravenous. The emotions of the last few hours had left him little room to realize what his body was feeling. "I like your plan, Jane. We'll meet you in the cafeteria."

Jane took off purposefully to find a phone as Matt turned Marta toward the elevator. Then they were alone in the elevator. Such luxury! Marta was leaning against him, her head touching his shoulder. He wrapped an arm around her.

"It's going to be all right, Marta. You're too tired right now to talk about anything in depth, but I want you to know I'm here for you. You come second only to the Lord with me."

She looked up into his eyes with a look of questioning wonder.

"I know it's too soon to talk like that, but I have to let you know. If you want me, I'm yours." He leaned down and laid his lips tenderly on hers. They suddenly realized that the elevator had stopped, the doors were open, and there were several people grinning at them. Matt felt the heat slowly seep into his face. He mumbled apologies as he led Marta quickly out of the elevator and down the hall to the cafeteria.

Marta's energy level seemed to pick up as they sipped coffee and ate muffins, waiting for Jane to join them. Matt made his decision. They might not have another chance at privacy for a long time.

"Marta, what I meant in the elevator. . ."

She smiled gentle encouragement at him.

"I ...I love you," he blurted it out like a kid on his first date. He saw a look of incredulous joy dawn in her eyes. She started to speak and then glanced at the doorway. Matt turned and saw Jane coming, inwardly groaning that their moment was interrupted before he could confirm anything with Marta. When would they ever get a chance to really talk?

Jane kept up a cheerful patter while they ate. Rusty found them as they were finishing up.

"Hi, Guys," Rusty greeted them cheerfully; "the boss got a hotel suite so we wouldn't have to go all the way back to Silverdale. Two of us get to stay with Marta; one can sleep while the other stands watch."

"Is there still a reason to be so guarded?" Marta asked in alarm.

Rusty turned to her, "We still want to be careful, but we got that Sergei fellow. The Coast Guard picked him up just before he drowned. Trying to swim with handcuffs on is really hard, did you know that?"

Matt laughed in spite of his exhausted and frustrated state. Rusty could lighten the worst situation.

"So, we figure we've got the chief bad guy. Matt, your friend Bob got home safely and received a friendly visit from his local FBI office. He has quite a story to tell, and I think our admonition to be circumspect will add a bit of spice as well. We picked up Peter at the airport trying to book a flight for sunny Mexico. I don't think he'd find a warm welcome after spilling his guts under FBI surveillance. He's probably safer with us. He's beginning to realize that now. Still, we don't know who all is involved, and we've kind of taken a stick to a hornet's nest. The residue in the containers on that ship indicated there'd been as much cocaine in them as coffee beans. What a deal those guys had going. The sniffer dogs get thrown off by the coffee beans, and the cargo goes on its way.

Matt, I have some good news and some bad news for you. The good news is you are still employed; the bad news is that you may not be for long if you don't get down to the office ASAP. I'm to drop you off there before I take these lovely ladies to the hotel. Yes, you are the lucky winner of a fine grilling by the boss, and I, your lowly servant, get to go to a hotel with two beautiful women. Sometimes life is not fair."

Matt groaned aloud. "I tell you now and for the record, my days with the FBI are numbered. If any of you would leave me alone with this woman," he nodded toward Marta, "for even five minutes, I could tell you just how numbered they are. So, I will see Marta to her room and tuck her in before anything else happens. If her answer to a very important question is in the affirmative, the FBI will receive my handwritten resignation when I walk through the office door."

"Hold on, Partner. We'll change the plan a bit, and you can cool down. First priority shall be a nice soft bed for this very tired young lady. We'll talk some sense into you, and then everything will be just fine."

"Matt," Jane put a cautioning hand on his arm, "this isn't the time. Both you and Marta are stretched to the limit emotionally. Let's get to the car. Marta's about to drop on her feet."

Matt realized how selfish he was being and relented. He wanted to push Marta into an answer right now for his own convenience. She hardly knew him. He'd never even dated her, and here he was trying to squeeze a promise of marriage from her.

"You're right. Let's go." He helped Marta up, realizing that she'd been absolutely silent during the exchange which so intimately involved her.

Rusty and Jane had been nice enough to let Matt and Marta have the back seat. She came into his arms and immediately fell asleep. Jane turned back, saw the situation, and gave Matt a sly grin. She wisely chose not to tease him. Marta slept all the way to the hotel and didn't wake when they stopped. Matt lifted her out of the car and carried her tenderly to her room. She moved only when the elevator arrived. She mumbled, and Matt leaned close to hear.

"Mmm...love you...mmm." She fell back into a deep sleep.

Matt had no way of knowing whether she meant him or Nicolai or worse, Timothy! He had to have patience. He laid her on the bed in the room Jane indicated.

"I'll take it from here," she said sternly. "You get yourself to the office and settle up with Frank. Matt, you think things through before you do anything rash, you hear me?"

"Yes, Mom," he grinned at her and stuck out his tongue.

"Professional, Matt," Rusty nodded seriously. "You should teach that particular gesture at Quantico."

"Right. I'll see you guys after the inquisition." He took one last look at the woman he loved, sleeping peacefully, and left to try to cement what he hoped would be their future together.

Matt walked into the office a few minutes later, and, as he expected, the receptionist told him to go straight to Frank's office. He took a deep breath before entering, preparing himself to end a career and hopefully begin a marriage. He entered and stood shocked in the doorway. There sat a tall, blond woman who had to be Tanya Alexander, Marta's KGB mother. He had no doubts. He turned a quizzical look on Frank who sat there grinning from ear to ear.

"Matt", Frank said cheerfully, "meet Tanya Borisova. She's with the Russian Consulate and has brought us a most interesting proposition. Have a seat, and I'll explain it to you."

A half an hour later, Matt sat too stunned to respond and watched Tanya leave to give Marta the same proposition.

CHAPTER EIGHTEEN

Matt had not seen Marta since he'd agreed to the wild proposition presented to him the night before in Frank's office. That proposition eliminated all barriers to a lifetime with Marta; in fact, their marriage would fit neatly into it. He ached to be alone with her, however, to explain that this opportunity was independent of his love for her.

She gave him as indecipherable look as they entered Nicolai's room with Tanya and Frank. She then turned her attention to her father. Nicolai was sitting up in his hospital bed devouring the morning newspaper. Matt was surprised at how well he looked considering the amount of blood he'd lost. He was further surprised at the tenderness he felt for this man. It had only been deepened by what he had learned from Frank and Tanya. He felt sure that the offer they brought would grant this man the dearest wish of his heart. It would also present him with a terrible challenge. Was he willing to risk his precious daughter once more?

"Good morning, Nicolai," Tanya greeted him in English, showing her intention to be totally open and honest. "We've come as a committee to make you an offer." Her eyes twinkled with mischief, "I know how much you dearly love committees."

This brought a gruff "Humph" and an exaggerated scowl from the bed. "So, you've finally come to tell me my fate? Good. I'm an old man. I can't wait forever."

Matt couldn't hold back a laugh. Nicolai trying to paint himself as a fragile old man was ridiculous. The memories of trying to keep up with him on the climb up the side of the freighter were still very fresh.

"Yes," Tanya crowed delightedly, "we've come to tell you your fate, should you choose to accept it. I've been in contact with the Ministry of the Interior in Moscow." Another "Humph" from the bed indicated Nicolai hadn't much more respect for ministries than he did for committees.

"As you know, the FBI and the Ministry of the Interior have something of a partnership formed of necessity due to the Russian organized crime networks gaining so much power in our home land. With the additional indicator from our recent experience that the networks are international and linking with other crime syndicates as well as terrorist groups, that partnership is even more critical. This is, however, no news to you. You've been trying to raise red flags for some time. The Ministry is also aware that you have operatives in key areas."

Nicolai rose up in alarm, but Tanya held up her hand to forestall an explosion.

"This is not a problem, I promise you. Both the Ministry and the FBI recognize they need your help and the help of your network. Both countries wish to acknowledge the tremendous contribution you and your people have made in risking your lives to hold back this horror that faces us."

Tanya paused a moment, swallowing several times. "We need you Nicolai. You've always said that we can't let the mad dogs win. If they get nuclear weapons or entrench themselves much more firmly in the international economy, they'll win. They're much, much too close."

It was obvious that Tanya had Nicolai's intense interest now. "The FBI and the Ministry want to go into partnership with you, Nicolai. They want to work with your network. I understand that you want to protect your people until you're sure of everyone's motives. It's a dangerous game, Nicolai. We've always known that. Your operatives know that too."

"So, two countries want me as a partner! I'm flattered. As you say, however, I have my reservations. I also have reasons to distrust. If I enter this partnership, there will be measures in place to protect my network. I must work with people whose loyalty to decency is beyond question."

"We'll trust your ability to determine questions of loyalty, Nicolai," Frank put in. "Your network is absolutely pristine. No one, as far as I can tell, knows who your people are. It is only by Tanya's admission and Matt's verification from what you told him that we even know it exists. The proof, however, that it is there is in the information you've given us through your daughter. It is a gift beyond price and has proven her loyalty to your cause without question. It has also brought from the State Department an offer of citizenship in the United States for both of you. You, Nicolai, are a true citizen of the world."

Nicolai turned a fond look toward Marta, drinking her in, her soft expression showing the return of his deep affection. "I am glad for Marta," Nicolai responded softly, "I know her heart is here."

Matt felt his fatherly glance and thrilled to the acknowledgment that he considered him the beloved of his daughter. "For myself, I may be citizen of the world, but my heart lies deep in Ukrainian soil. How does the Ministry of the Interior and the FBI feel about that?"

"That is most important to both of us," Frank answered for himself and Tanya, who nodded to show her agreement. "The Ukraine is strategically critical for a number of reasons. We really hope you'll establish an economic center there that will rival those of the crime lords. That is what you'd planned isn't it? I understand you've established a number of people in entrepreneurial enterprises in every corner of the former Soviet Union to build an economic power base that could push the crime organizations back and provide people with legal options so the black market would lose much of its power. I also understand that KGB training comes in handy in defending those enterprises. You had personally planned to return to the Ukraine when things were settled here and when Marta was safe, right?"

Nicolai nodded, glancing from Matt to Tanya as if to say they'd talked too much. Matt felt himself blushing, but Nicolai understood that as an FBI agent he had been required to give a complete disclosure and debriefing.

Tanya then took up the pitch, "What the American offer means, Nicolai, is a choice. You do not have to cooperate with us. That's what they are saying. The Ministry of the Interior also wishes you to know that they want your voluntary cooperation. Should you not wish to give it, they are willing to give you free reign on the assumption that you'll be effective no matter what methodology you choose to follow. They are somewhat impressed with you, Old Friend."

"And what makes them think I want to do anything but go home and grow wheat? That is my dream," Nicolai chuckled.

Tanya gave him a withering look, but before she could say anything Marta surprised them all by entering the discussion.

"Papa," Nicolai's eyes filled with tears at that term of endearment from his daughter's lips, "would it help you to decide what to do if I told you I'll be working with this partnership? Oh, I'm accepting American citizenship. That has always been my dream, but I'll be working with the Ministry and the FBI in the Moscow office where Matt will soon be assigned."

Matt's heart soared with hope, and he felt a grin growing on his face as the light dawned for Nicolai. They were going to be a team.

"I, too, Nicolai," Tanya added, to let him know that the team would be complete.

An awestruck Nicolai looked at Frank. "You are a man of prayer?" he asked Frank, who nodded. "I believe you are seeing a miracle. This is an answer to a prayer I never dared utter, for it seemed beyond all hope."

Matt's heart thrilled with the hope that a door was opening in Nicolai.

"I could ask for no better team. These will be my allies and the ones I will trust with my network. Understand, I do you no favors. By entrusting you with this information, I put your lives in grave danger. Are you staying here?" he asked Frank.

"Yes, I'll be the stateside control for the operation."

"I want you also to hold the information in case something happens in the field. I can't believe I'm doing this. My own daughter, for whom I risked everything, is now pulled into the gravest danger. Yet, My Love, I cannot hold you safe. The world is simply not a safe place. But you must have some refresher training. . .aiiee! I thought I taught you better." Nicolai's grin broke the tension with exaggerated humor. Marta beamed at being teased by her father.

"But since you've shown yourself to be of almost suicidal courage," he frowned in mock ferocity, "I suppose there will be no stopping you. At least there is another watch dog, eh?" Nicolai looked slyly at Matt. There could be no doubt in anyone's mind now about who held Matt Barton's heart in her hand, but did he hold hers? He glanced nervously at Marta, who was blushing. His heart went into overdrive.

"So, we're in agreement?" Frank broke into the moment with his usual sensitivity to underlying emotion. Matt was glad for a return to the business at hand. He wanted to ensure that Marta understood that his wish for a personal relationship had nothing to do with the business relationship they would have as teammates in the field.

"We have an agreement subject to my approval of the details of our operation." Nicolai responded firmly, all business once again.

"Of course," Frank acknowledged one professional to another. "I also want you to know I'm honored that you're willing to trust me to be your fail-safe with the network."

The nurse came in then and asked them to leave, saying that Mr. Gorgonov needed his rest. Marta stopped quickly by his bed to give him a daughter's kiss. Tanya was the last to file out of the room. Matt thought he might soon be able to repay Nicky's teasing if Tanya's look of love was any indication of things to come. He just hoped he'd be doing that teasing as his son-in-law.

"Marta," he called as they stepped out of Nicolai's room. She turned to him with almost a hunted look, and Matt's heart constricted with fear.

Marta had left her father's hospital room with a heart full of wonder and questions. Everyone seemed to make assumptions about her relationship with Matt, but they'd never been alone long enough for her to be certain of his feelings and expectations. He had told her that he loved her, but she needed to hear more. She looked nervously at Matt. She was so uptight; she jumped when Frank spoke from her other side.

"Matt, I imagine you and Marta have some things to talk over." She turned to see a soft smile on the man's face. "Why don't you take the afternoon off? Oh, and you might want to get some sleep sometime in the next twenty-four hours. You look awful."

"Marta," she jumped again at Matt's voice. "Would you have lunch with me?" Matt sounded almost shy. She nodded and followed him out of the hospital and to a car. He opened and held the door for her as if she were royalty.

Once he had her settled in the car, he began, "I know this offer is all very sudden. This is probably not the time or the place to talk about...well, us. I mean, you've already made one big decision today. I've made a couple of big decisions, too. I decided when I left you asleep yesterday morning that I was going to quit the FBI."

"Oh, no, Matt. You can't," Marta panicked. What could he mean? They were going to Moscow together. If he quit, they couldn't be together.

"Now, hear me out," he said in a calming voice. "At that time I was sure the FBI wouldn't let me marry anyone who'd been a KGB agent."

Marta gave a little gasp, and Matt gave her a sideways glance, obviously trying with no success to see both her and the traffic. "This is a dumb place to have this conversation. Let me pull off, and we'll park and talk this out." He signaled and pulled over into a metered parking space. "Let me feed the machine," he grinned and jumped out, change in hand. He was laughing when he returned. "Isn't this typical of us. Here I am trying to propose and a parking meter takes precedence."

"You're trying to propose?" Marta asked breathlessly.

"Clumsily, but that's what I'm trying to do. I want you to know I want to marry you whether we do the Moscow assignment together or not. I mean, you're free to make whatever choice you want without regard to the assignment. I'll still quit the FBI if you want me to, and we could go grow wheat with Nicky or something."

Marta laid her hand on his arm.

"Yes."

"What?" Matt looked at her in surprise.

"I said, yes. I'll marry you. You were eventually going to ask that, weren't you?"

"Are you sure, Marta? I mean you just had your first date, and it wasn't even with me."

"I'm very sure. I just had my first kiss, too, and it was with you. All I've wanted since then was for you to repeat it."

And he did.

EPILOGUE

Matt turned toward the back of the church as the members of the congregation came to their feet in honor of the bride. The shining white vision she made took his breath away. Dressed in simple white satin with a flowing white veil, her raven hair cascading in curls underneath, she was coming closer and closer, her eyes fixed on him. Matt forced himself to breath. This woman was actually giving herself to him. What had he done to deserve this?

Marta felt Matt's golden gaze on her. She sensed her father's strength as she leaned on his arm, amazed at how quickly he had recovered to fulfill this joyous duty. She gripped her great-grandmother's Bible instead of a bouquet of flowers. Matt reached out to her in an involuntary gesture as she drew up next to him. Her father gently put her hand into her groom's and temporarily retrieved the Bible. For just a moment she watched as her papa moved away to sit beside Tanya. She turned back to see the deep tenderness on Matt's strong face. The vows passed in a golden fog. She responded as they had rehearsed the day before. Then Matt lifted her veil and drew her into their joining kiss. The universe stood still as God joined together what no man could put asunder.

THE BEGINNING